Invitation from Bali

You are cordially invited to...

...a destination wedding! For estranged brothers Ben and Will, the unexpected invitation to celebrate their mother's whirlwind marriage brings up challenges—and feelings—they're unprepared for.

For Ben, having best friend Charlotte by his side is all he needs to cope with his family's drama. But amid tropical cocktails, the shimmering turquoise sea and fabulous sunsets, something between Ben and Charlotte shifts... It breaks all the rules of their friendship, but could it be worth the risk?

Will needs a plus-one and waitress Summer is the perfect candidate. Why? Because they're complete opposites! Tightly wound Will is all business, while free-spirited Summer is ready for adventure. Which means their watertight contract of pretending to be in love but not actually falling for each other is a deal they can stick to...right?

As warm Bali days lead to hot Bali nights, one thing's for sure—the lives of the Watson brothers will never be the same again!

Enjoy Ben and Charlotte's story

Breaking the Best Friend Rule

Available now!

And look out for Will and Summer's story

The Billionaire's Plus-One Deal

Coming soon!

Dear Reader,

The friends-to-lovers trope is one of my favorites to read, but I've always found it challenging to write. If two gorgeous people are good friends, then doesn't it stand to reason they also fall in love?

You'd think so, but this pair, Ben and Charlotte, stubbornly refuse to. Charlotte's fiancé died in an accident several years ago, and even though she promised him she'd find love again, it has proven elusive. She runs from any prospective relationship before she gets too close.

Ben knows that Charlotte isn't over her fiancé, so is guarded with his own heart. The last thing he wants to be is runner-up in anyone's affections.

Some Bali sunshine and a family wedding might be just the thing to make them see sense!

This is also my first duet—in Bali Ben has to deal with his estranged brother, Will, who will have his own chance to shine in book two of the Invitation from Bali series.

I hope you enjoy your escape in the tropical sunshine.

Justine
xx

Breaking the Best Friend Rule

—

Justine Lewis

Recycling programs for this product may not exist in your area.

ISBN-13: 978-1-335-59664-2

Breaking the Best Friend Rule

Copyright © 2024 by Justine Lewis

For questions and comments about the quality of this book, please contact us at CustomerService@Harlequin.com.

Harlequin Enterprises ULC
22 Adelaide St. West, 41st Floor
Toronto, Ontario M5H 4E3, Canada
www.Harlequin.com

Printed in U.S.A.

Justine Lewis writes uplifting, heartwarming contemporary romances. She lives in Australia with her hero husband, two teenagers and an outgoing puppy. When she isn't writing, she loves to walk her dog in the bush near her house, attempt to keep her garden alive and search for the perfect frock. She loves hearing from readers, and you can visit her at justinelewis.com.

Books by Justine Lewis

Harlequin Romance

Billionaire's Snowbound Marriage Reunion
Fiji Escape with Her Boss
Back in the Greek Tycoon's World
Beauty and the Playboy Prince

Visit the Author Profile page
at Harlequin.com.

For my amazing daughter, Emily,
who brings me joy every day.

CHAPTER ONE

THE RAIN ALWAYS made Charlotte nervous. Today's torrential downpour, with water coming down in sheets and overflowing gutters, positively made her heart race. It was good weather for ducks. For the garden. And getting into fatal accidents.

She was safe in her gallery, she told herself. *Her* gallery. An old but light-filled space on a quiet Soho side street. She would have preferred a more prominent position to attract passers-by but could barely afford the rent on this space as it was. Though three years after opening she was still solvent, which was more than many commercial art galleries could say.

Customers didn't tend to wander past without purpose on days like this, so the afternoon was dragging. At times she fancied the clock was standing still. She tried to keep herself busy by digging around on the Internet for up-and-coming artists. The principle of her gallery was to find yet-to-be-discovered artists and help them on the journey to grow their careers, rather than chasing after already established names. It was a model that had proven to be successful and canny investors sought out her gallery and her advice. The bigger galleries watched her carefully.

A crack of thunder made her jump. She tried to take her mind off it by sending some emails, but her heart rate remained high.

The old wooden-framed glass door rattled open and her best friend, Ben Watson, appeared, soaking wet but carrying two coffees from the cafe across the street.

'Sorry,' he muttered as he shook his long, wet brown hair from his eyes, leaving a Ben-sized puddle on the floor.

Charlotte raced to the back office, retrieved a towel she kept on hand and passed it to him. He wiped his face, beard and hair and then hung his wet coat on the rack.

'Why are you out in this weather? By choice?'

Ben's apartment and studio were in Camden. He might still be in it, safe and warm. Working on his latest piece. Something was up.

'I came to bring you coffee,' he replied, passing her one of the cups.

'I'm grateful. But really?' Other people didn't hate the rain as much as Charlotte, but most didn't wander around in it without a good reason.

'No, I do have an ulterior motive. Something's um…happened.'

Ben's usually happy face looked tight. Concerned. The last time she'd seen him like this was just before he returned to Australia to see his father, who had suffered a massive and unexpected stroke. His father had passed away before Ben's plane landed back in Adelaide.

'Oh, no. What's going on?'

He sipped his coffee. His blue eyes were cast downwards, and his wet hair now slicked back off his forehead, which was furrowed. 'If you get an invitation to your mother's wedding less than two weeks before the event, are you even really invited?' he asked.

'Your mother's getting married? I didn't even know she was dating anyone.'

'Nor did I,' he said darkly.

Charlotte did a quick calculation. It had been just over a year since Ben's father, David, had passed away, the September before last.

Ben's parents had been married for the best part of forty years. Charlotte hadn't met either of them. Ben rarely returned to his native Australia since leaving it at the age of twenty-one to pursue his artistic ambitions overseas and his parents had never visited him here, in London. Ben adored his mother, but his relationship with his business-focused father had always been tense. As had his relationship with his older brother, Will. Will had gone into the family business and neither Will nor his father had supported Ben's dreams of being an artist.

Charlotte suspected that most days Ben didn't

give either his father or brother a second thought, but the old wounds were never far beneath the surface, especially when something like this happened.

Charlotte motioned to a seat and Ben sat down beside Charlotte's desk.

'Who's she marrying?' she asked.

Ben took out his phone, brought up a photo, and passed it to Charlotte. It was a photo of a happy couple standing near the ocean, the man's arm wrapped around the woman's shoulders, both beaming at one another, oblivious to the person taking the photo. Charlotte recognised the smiling woman as Ben's mother, Diane. The man was at least a foot taller than her and very handsome, but she didn't say that to Ben.

Instead she tried to find the right word. 'He looks…'

'Young?' Ben said.

'I was going to say hot.'

Ben glared at her.

'Sorry, but he is. Young and hot.'

'It's hard to tell from the photograph alone. I've looked him up. He's forty-seven. Fourteen years younger than Mum.'

Go Diane, Charlotte thought, but kept the opinion to herself.

'Half the age of the oldest person, plus seven. Isn't that the rule? So they're well within that.'

Over the four years they had known one another, Ben and Charlotte had discussed all of life's important questions, including who made the best coffee—Australians—the best way to end a relationship—quickly, clearly and politely—and what amounted to an inappropriate age gap in a couple.

Ben frowned. 'I'm not sure that rule applies to one's mother.'

'But forty-seven isn't that young. At least he's older than you.'

Ben dragged his hand through his still wet hair, slicking it back even further. He looked like a drowned dog, and sad eyes completed the picture. But no wonder, his mother remarrying so soon after his father's death and giving Ben practically no notice of the nuptials. Her chest ached for him.

'I'm not worried about his age,' Ben said.

'His hotness?'

Ben grimaced.

Perhaps this wasn't the right moment to tease him.

'It's not his age that's worrying me. Or even his...' Ben waved his hand over his phone. 'Or even his attractiveness. It just seems so quick.'

Charlotte agreed. A year did seem a little fast to be finding a new husband after the death of your husband of forty-odd years.

Charlotte's first and last serious boyfriend, Tim, had passed away seven years ago and she was yet to meet a man she could contemplate staying with for more than a few weeks, let alone marrying. People told her that she had mourned long enough, and her reply was always that people mourn at different rates. It seemed like an apt reply now, for the opposite reason.

'Did you even know she was seeing him?' she asked.

'I had no idea, but then I haven't been back to Adelaide since the funeral.'

'So the first you're hearing about her relationship with this man is the wedding invitation? Gosh.'

Charlotte had thought that Ben's difficulties had just been between his father and his brother, Will. She'd always believed Ben was on good terms with his mother. This news must be making him wonder about all sorts of things.

'It's my fault. I guess I wasn't around after Dad passed. I haven't been there for her, like I should've been.'

'Maybe not, but you came back to London with her blessing. You talk regularly, don't you?'

Ben nodded.

Younger man, older, richer but emotionally vulnerable woman. There was another theory they should canvas.

'Are you worried that maybe he's using her? That he's after her money?'

'Even if I was, it would hardly be my business to say. My father made it very clear I gave up any rights to the family business when I moved away. Besides, Dad was so tight about his money and Will's just the same. So much of it is tied up in trusts and other arrangements.'

'But she's still wealthy, isn't she?'

'Yes, but I don't even have to ask to know that Will must have insisted on an airtight prenup.'

'But it's not his money, surely? She must have her own money that your dad left her. Will can't be controlling her fortune.'

'I wouldn't put it past him.'

Charlotte bit her tongue. She'd never met Will, Ben's older and—according to Ben—super-uptight brother. When Ben declared his wish to go to art school, instead of work in the family company, his brother and father ended all financial support for him. However, being forced to work his way through life and support himself had made Ben focused and single-minded. He was now a highly successful painter, whose work was shown in galleries all over the world. Ben had found financial security and success his own way and Charlotte knew he was immensely proud that he'd done it on his own terms.

'Then what is it? What's really worrying you?'

The two old friends could speak honestly and openly with one another. He was more straightforward than any of her girlfriends, but no less close to her. She valued his advice and counsel and knew he did the same of her. Thankfully, she wasn't attracted to Ben nor he to her and their friendship was stronger and more solid because of it. Friendships she'd had with other men had been ruined in the past when either she or he had become attracted to the other. Charlotte was glad that neither she nor Ben had ever developed complicated feelings towards the other.

'I thought they loved one another,' Ben said, sagging. 'I mean, I know Dad was difficult, of course he was, but I thought Mum loved him. But what if she didn't? I mean, what if all this time she was actually desperately unhappy? Like I said, he wasn't an easy man to love.'

'Ahh. Right.'

Even though Charlotte had struggled after losing Tim, she did know that people dealt with grief differently.

'It is so soon,' Ben said.

'This doesn't mean she didn't love your father. Or that she was unhappy. Forty years is a long time to be married to someone. Just because she's found new happiness it doesn't mean what she had was any less special.'

Charlotte grasped the pendant around her neck and turned it between her fingers. The feel of the smooth, shiny silver between her fingertips always reminded her of Tim and centred her when she was uneasy.

'You can find new love without dishonouring the old.' Charlotte said the words, almost a repetition of what her mother kept saying to her, but her heart wasn't in it.

Ben raised a suspicious eyebrow, as though he didn't believe she was committed to the sentiment either.

'Why don't you just wait and talk to her? Reserve judgement before you meet him.'

'The wedding's in ten days! How much time will I actually get to know him? That's if I even go. This invitation? Is it a real invitation? Is she expecting me to come halfway around the world with so little notice? What's all that about?'

'Maybe…' Charlotte was lost for words. Ten days did seem unnecessarily hasty.

'See, you can't think of a good reason either,' Ben replied.

Maybe she couldn't at this moment, but she didn't want to discount the possibility that Diane might have a good reason for getting married so quickly. Even if she didn't, this wedding was an important life event and if Ben didn't go because of old wounds, or confusion or hurt or whatever reason, he'd regret it.

'She's your mother. You will go, won't you?'

Ben sighed. 'I don't know.'

'When were the invitations sent?'

'This morning. By email. Also, it's in Bali.'

'Bali? The island?'

He nodded. 'Bali, the island. In Indonesia. On the other side of the world.'

Charlotte had never been to Bali. It sounded warm, relaxing. She imagined friendly people, vibrant jungle and crystal-clear water. It probably had great food too, tasty spices and fragrant herbs. She began to salivate.

'Well, I think you should go. Even if she isn't expecting you to come, I think you should.' Charlotte looked out of the window at the grey London afternoon. 'Apart from anything it's a holiday. It'll be warm!' She'd do anything for a chance to escape the wet London autumn. Even go to an excruciatingly awkward family wedding. To feel sand between her toes. 'And I'll come with you.'

The words were out of her mouth before she'd thought twice. But she didn't regret them for a second.

Ben's eyes widened.

'You will? You don't have to.'

Her offer had been quick, but she was sure. Ben was her best friend and had been so supportive and helpful to her over the past few years: with advice on her gallery, cooking her warm meals, not to mention being a non-judgemental listener when she had to tell someone about her latest dating misstep.

'No, I really want to go. I want to be there for you.'

She couldn't read the look on Ben's face and tell if he was relieved at her offer or pained by it.

'And come on, Bali! A break in the sun! Won't that be great, with or without a wedding?'

He frowned. 'They're getting there in three days' time. Three days! That's no notice at all. It takes nearly a day to fly there.'

'So, we leave in two days.'

'Don't you want to go to the exhibition at the Royal College?'

She did, especially as it would be full of work by recent graduates and an opportunity to spot new talent before anyone else did.

'So we leave the day after that.'

'And the gallery?' Ben looked around. 'Who'll look after it?'

'Marcia can manage it for a week. Besides, this is an opportunity to travel, maybe find some new artists too. Ben, it's so perfect. We have to go.'

'Okay, but let me book.' He crossed his arms. She wanted to giggle. He was trying to look firm, but he was still soaked and looked as if he'd been dragged out of a pond.

'Fine, but I'll pay you back.' She crossed her arms back and stood with her legs apart to let him know she was serious too.

Ben shook his head, but she didn't know if the shake meant, 'Of course you will pay me back' or 'I will definitely shout you'.

She'd argue about it later. Right now he was upset and stressed.

With his hair slicked back, she could see more

of Ben's face than usual. He hid behind a brown beard, which in Charlotte's opinion was way too long, and wavy brown hair that was always in need of a cut. He had a distracted artist thing going on, with loose, fraying sweaters, dirty boots and hands that were perpetually splattered with paint. His dishevelled appearance didn't hurt his reputation, only seemed to enhance it. Ben was one of the most sought-after artists in London at the moment. Charlotte mused: talented men could get away with ignoring their appearance in a way that women couldn't. But under his apparently chaotic appearance, Ben was her rock. Solid, unflappable. The only time she'd seen him shaken was when his father had died.

And now.

The rain had eased by the time Ben left, as had her mood. She was going to Bali! Getting away from London at the time of the anniversary was a truly excellent idea. Escaping the wet cold British autumn for the sunny skies and warmth of a tropical island was such an obvious solution to her October funk she should have thought of it years ago. A few customers started wandering in and by the time she was closing up that evening the skies had cleared.

Warm, tropical. That was all she knew about Bali, but that was enough.

October was always hard in London. The change of season. The rain.

It had been a soaking October day when Tim had had his accident, sliding off his motorbike under a poorly timed lorry.

The accident had been quick, but the end hadn't been. He'd had several major surgeries, been in so much pain for weeks, before his body decided it had really had too much.

They had both been twenty-three.

She'd moved on slowly. In his last days, when it had looked as if his body was just not going to be strong enough to fight off the injuries and subsequent infections, he'd made her promise she'd find love again. But a second love had been elusive for Charlotte.

No one was quite like her Tim.

She tried though; if there was a man she could love as much as Tim, she was going to find him. She dated many men. So many her girlfriends rolled their eyes and her mother shook her head.

Only Ben didn't judge, and he understood why she always seemed to end things after a few dates. Ben had watched over her for the past four years, like a big brother. Not the super-protective older brother though, but a cool, watch-from-a-non-embarrassing-distance type of brother. Close enough to be there at short notice if things got uncomfortable. And always there to listen to her talk about any fallout afterwards. A perpetual singleton like herself, Ben understood the risks of committing too quickly to anything and why she was so cautious.

Yes, she had to go to Bali for Ben. He had always been there for her.

Her flat was only a few Tube stops away and she wanted to get home and start googling swimsuits. She had tentative plans to have a drink with a guy she'd met at a party a week ago—Dale? Dan? No, Don. The fact that she couldn't even remember his name was an obvious clue that it wasn't likely to be a date that would change her life. She sent him a message to cancel.

Hi Don. I'm so sorry, but something has come up and I have to go abroad for a bit. It's probably best that we don't start something I can't finish. C xx

Her usual sign-off. Her friends told her that she should just make it a signature block on her messages: Sorry, but I don't think we should start something we can't finish.

She meant it to be kind, to let the poor fella down easily. Let him know that she didn't want anything serious. She was under no obligation to commence a relationship with anyone.

Don replied right away.

Safe travels. Let me know if you want to catch up when you're back.

She sighed. Don was probably one of the nice ones. Just not the right nice one for her.

At home, she took off her high-heeled boots, skirt and bra, changed into sweats and made herself comfortable on the couch with her laptop.

She'd opened a browser and typed in 'tropical getaway swimsuits' when her phone pinged with a message from Ben. It was a link to a plane ticket from Heathrow to Denpasar, leaving in three days' time. She messaged him right back.

Business class! Ben!

It's a twenty-hour trip. Trust me, we'll need it. And I AM PAYING.

Are you sure? I didn't expect you to buy business class seats!

Do you want me to leave you in cattle class while I sip champers in business?

Charlotte was comfortable, but not so comfortable she could drop thousands of dollars on last-minute business class seats to Bali. It was so generous of Ben she hardly knew what to say so she simply typed XXX and clutched her phone to her chest.

Seconds later he messaged back.

You're doing me a favour. I'm really glad you're coming with me.

* * *

The exhibition was in a gallery in East London, featuring work of current and former students. Like all such exhibitions, the works were of wildly differing styles and quality. Ben's eyes were drawn to Charlotte right away. She was wearing a long, bright green jacket, a fitted black jumpsuit and bright red heels. She looked stunning, as usual.

She was studying a canvas that filled half a wall. He grabbed two glasses of champagne from a nearby waiter and walked over to her.

Charlotte was just the type of woman Ben could have fallen for, if he hadn't stopped himself, just in time. Because what business would someone as wonderful as Charlotte have falling in love with him?

Minutes into their first meeting he'd found himself drawn to her. They had met at a mutual friend's party, and she had stood next to him in a corner of a cramped terrace, where, for some reason he couldn't remember, she'd told him exactly what she thought about Picasso and his treatment of women, waving her hands around and nearly splashing her drink over him. Her beauty was obvious: long straight dark hair flowed down her back, colour high in her cheeks, naturally defining them. She stood straight and confidently.

Her intelligence was almost as quickly apparent as her beauty. Her dark blue eyes flashed with insight and thoughts about the world. Her passion for art came across next, which would have endeared her to Ben in any event. But it was their shared gently cynical sense of humour and appreciation of the ridiculous that he really adored.

Now, four years later and on the other side of London, he stood with Charlotte looking at a work by an artist he'd never seen before. The work was competent, but uninspired. He handed her one of the glasses.

'Are you all set for tomorrow?' he asked, knowing full well that she wouldn't be packed and that her flat would look as though it had been ransacked by a burglar.

Outwardly, Charlotte looked sleek and well put together. It was a mystery to him how such a well-presented creature managed to emerge from her messy flat each day. But that was Charlotte.

He was the opposite; he liked the spaces around him to be tidy and ordered but outwardly he was, as Charlotte called him, a bit of a scruff. He rubbed his beard. He couldn't even remember the last time he'd had a haircut.

Together, they would have made one put-together person.

She narrowed her eyes at him. 'I'll be ready. Besides, it won't take me long. We're going to Bali. A couple of bikinis and a dress for the wedding and I'll be set.'

Ben imagined Charlotte in a bikini and swallowed hard, quickly shaking the image away. He didn't think about Charlotte like that. He had built a wall around those thoughts. It was high and he didn't look over it. Let alone try to scale it.

The night they'd first met he'd been working up the courage to subtly ask if she was single, when another man had joined their conversation and completely monopolised Charlotte, charming her with stories about a recent trip he'd taken to Florence.

They had wandered away together and Ben had taken himself home, miffed.

Hadn't they got along well? There had been a spark, at least on his side. But no, she'd wandered away with some Lothario, old enough to be her father, and left Ben feeling confused and empty.

He'd run into Charlotte at an exhibition a week later; the art scene in London was big, but still small enough that you did come across the same faces. This time she'd approached him. She'd confessed she was scouting him out to see if he wanted to exhibit in her new space and they'd gone for coffee. They'd talked for hours, but this time, as prospective business associates, he'd been careful to stay professional. He wasn't going to play runner-up to the charmer she'd left with the other night. Or to any of the steady stream of men Charlotte seemed to date.

And then there was the night she'd told him all about Tim. A few months into their acquaintanceship he'd found her, after leaving a function, standing in a doorway, not moving. It had been raining heavily and he'd offered her use of his umbrella, but she'd refused. She'd grabbed his arm and held him back and they'd waited under the awning together until the rain had passed. It had been then that she'd told him all about Tim and the accident. From that point on Ben had realised Charlotte's heart was not free and his own heart would be safest locked away.

Because, despite what Charlotte might claim until she was out of breath, she wasn't ready for another relationship. The pattern quickly became apparent to Ben: Charlotte would meet a man—sometimes on an app, sometimes at a party, sometimes through work—and they would hit it off. Charlotte was beautiful, charming and great company. Men were attracted to her like bees to pollen. They would have a few dates—three was usually the limit but once or twice some poor fella had made it to four—and then Charlotte would pull back. Either because she could tell the man was not for her, or, sometimes, because she thought he might be. The thought of falling in love scared Charlotte so much that she had occasionally ended new relationships when she'd felt herself feeling more about the man. Charlotte didn't have any intention—consciously or otherwise—of falling in love with any of them.

And she told Ben about every single one of

them. Where they went, what had been said, what she didn't like about the guy. If he *had* fallen for Charlotte, the last few years of his life would have been an utter misery. He knew that by keeping their relationship platonic he'd ensured that she would never push him away. By staying her friend, he would always have Charlotte in his life. And that felt like a win.

'What do you think?' Ben nodded to the painting they were standing in front of.

'Competent, but he's not telling me anything I don't already know.'

Ben smiled to himself. They almost always agreed on art. It was an unusually slick exhibition for recent students. The champagne was above par and there was a string quartet as well.

'I love strings,' Ben confessed.

'Really? I never knew that.' Charlotte tilted her head and studied him closely for a second. He felt his cheeks warm; that would be the champagne kicking in.

'There are lots of things you don't know about me.' He said it in a way that was half teasing, half trying to be enigmatic.

'Nonsense. I know you,' she said.

She did.

And she didn't. She knew more about him than anyone else on earth. But there was still a part of him that was locked behind a high brick wall that was impossible for even her to scale.

'Have you spoken to your mother?' she asked.

'Briefly. She's thrilled you're coming too.' Diane had gently prodded him for details about his relationship with Charlotte over the years, questions that Ben had simply rebuffed. But this time the questioning had been pointed.

'I've arranged you a one-bedroom villa. Will that be fine?' she'd asked.

'We'll each need a bedroom, Mum. I'll call them.'

'No, no, I'll take care of it,' she'd said, and he hoped that she had. Charlotte would not thank him if they arrived to find one bed waiting for them. If that was the case, he'd be on the floor.

'I hope I'm not intruding on a family occasion,' she said.

'Not at all. Besides, by the sounds of things there will be quite a few people there. I assumed it was some sort of elopement, but Gus's family and friends will be there as well.'

Given it was going to be quite a big affair, Ben still wondered what the rush was, but that was something he'd have to ask his mother face to face. Maybe it was Gus's idea, get everything tied up before Diane had second thoughts. Before Will could get the seal on the prenup. He knew he could call his brother and ask what was going on, but the thought of picking up the phone and dialling his brother's number made his mouth dry.

Maybe they love one another?

Ben felt like scoffing. Love? Did love really make you crazy or did people simply use it as an excuse for bad decisions? Ben had never met a feeling he couldn't analyse, unpack and use for his art. He'd never let his feelings for someone lead him to do anything reckless.

He supposed that was one thing he had in common with his brother.

As though she could see straight into his skull, Charlotte said, 'I'm looking forward to meeting Will.'

Ben's spine straightened at the mention of his brother's name. And the fact that he had piqued Charlotte's interest.

'What's the matter? He's your brother. I'm curious.'

'Nothing's the matter. But we're not at all alike.'

'Sure, sure, but you're brothers, close in age. Same parents. How different can you be?'

'Very.'

Eighteen months could make a lot of difference. Will was the golden boy. His father's favourite. Ben was an afterthought. A disappointment. He lacked his father's aptitude for numbers and his love of large ones, particularly those numbers with a dollar sign in front of them, whereas Will shared his father's passion for money and accumulating it.

Ben didn't understand their obsession and was called ungrateful and spoilt because of it. His father had never understood that Ben was never un-grateful, he would just rather be thinking about the way the world worked and studying how things looked and why. And most of all he loved creating and shaping things with his hands. Rather than keeping track of how much money he'd made.

Ben was well aware he'd benefited from his family's fortune: it had paid for his private school education. But his father had paid for Will's uni-versity tuition and refused point-blank to pay for Ben to attend art school. When Will had gradu-ated, not only were his fees paid, but his father had bought Will a new car and an apartment of his own. He told Ben that Will deserved all those things because Will was working for him, but Ben always knew it was an excuse.

Ben had enjoyed a very privileged upbringing and lived at home while he studied. He'd never gone hungry, but it still smarted. Not the lack of money, but the love and respect the money rep-resented.

Ben had worked through university, bartend-ing, teaching high-school students and occasion-ally receiving secret handouts from his mother. Finally, at twenty-one, he'd completed his degree, with first class honours and the year prize.

His father had come, grimacing, to the gradu-ation exhibition, literally dragged along by the hand by Diane.

'What a waste of time and money,' his father had said when he'd walked through the exhibition.

But someone didn't think Ben's art was a waste of money. *Someone* had paid the ludicrously high price Ben had placed on his prize-winning painting of his favourite beach. The painting had been commended for its unusual use of perspective and he'd been personally proud of the way he'd used the colour to evoke the mood. He loved that painting and had set the price at an exorbitant amount of ten thousand dollars, expecting no one to pay it and for him to be able to keep it.

To his amazement, a red sticker had been placed on the work early in the evening. The next day Ben had bought a plane ticket with the money he'd made selling that painting, flown to Los Angeles and never looked back. Since that day he had supported himself entirely, without a further cent from his family.

He was sometimes sad that he'd sold that painting to an anonymous investor, he'd loved it so much, but the fact that someone had been willing to pay him ten thousand dollars for something he'd painted had given him the courage to launch himself into the world. It made him proud to know that somewhere out there that painting was making someone happy. Ben had his whole career to thank them for, really.

Particularly his life in London, which he loved. Los Angeles had been busy and vibrant. Then he'd moved on to New York, which had been exciting, but exhausting. In London he'd found a happy medium. Busy, crowded, the meeting place of the world. A magnet for all cultures.

London was confident, with statesman-like vistas, and history that caught in your throat. It wasn't as overtly beautiful as Paris or Venice, but it still had buildings that could take your breath away, laneways that would make you swoon and streets you wanted to dance along.

And above all, London had Charlotte.

At some point in his reverie she'd wandered off to look at another painting and had begun chatting to another man.

He watched from a distance, curious about what would transpire, but confident in the knowledge that tomorrow she would be getting on a plane with him.

CHAPTER TWO

WHEN THE CAR pulled up at the kerb Charlotte wheeled her suitcase towards it. Ben jumped out to help her with her bag and she did a double take.

What on earth?

Ben looked down and rubbed his bare chin subconsciously. 'Yeah, I know. I just got it done this morning. Is it awful?'

She looked at her best friend as if seeing him for the first time. She was so accustomed to seeing the bottom half of his face covered with a thick clump of soft brown hair it took her a moment to unscramble the new image before her.

'It's awful, isn't it? You hate it,' he said, groaning.

'No, not at all,' she said quickly. 'It's just different. Give me a moment to catch up.'

He lifted her case into the boot and closed it. They both slid into the back seat of the car and the driver pulled from the kerb.

She stole sideways glances at him. 'Why?' she asked.

'The heat.'

'Really? How hot will it be?'

'Hot.'

Without whiskers obscuring it, she could see his Adam's apple rise and fall as he swallowed, probably pushing down his anxiety about seeing his mother again.

It was the first time Ben would see his family since returning briefly for his father's funeral a year ago. Charlotte hadn't gone with him on that trip, but he'd been different since his return. Not a big change, only something that she, as his closest friend, had noticed. A sadness, partly, but also a deeper maturity. Charlotte had never lost a parent so she could only imagine that was what it was. She also knew that Ben's feelings towards his family were complicated—part anger, part guilt. They had never understood his passion—or rather his *need*—to paint. Those who were not artists often didn't, but surely a parent only wanted their children to be happy and fulfilled? Apparently, Ben's father had not, and Ben hadn't had the opportunity to make his peace with his father before his death.

She knew Ben didn't regret moving away though, breaking free from the Watson empire. He had been born an artist and so he'd had to leave in order to pursue his goals. It had taken a lot of courage to break free from his family's expectations, but that didn't mean he didn't feel some guilt about not being around to help with the family business, be a part of it.

Charlotte was immensely grateful for her own parents, who had encouraged to her to follow her passion and to study fine arts and art history. They were proud of her, and they also adored Ben.

'What did Don say when you told him you were going away for a week?' Ben asked. 'Or didn't you tell him?'

'Of course I told him, I sent him a message. And I told him it probably wouldn't work out with us.'

Ben nodded.

'Don't say it,' she said.

'I wasn't going to say anything.'

'But you're thinking, *She's dumped another guy.*'

'That's not at all what I was thinking.'

'What were you thinking?'

'I was thinking that at least you let the poor guy know. At least you didn't ghost him.'

'I always let them know,' she said. That was a half-truth. Sometimes she didn't call or message back. Particularly if the guy in question had been rude.

Ben smirked.

'There's nothing wrong with not messaging back. I'm only doing what millions of guys have done over the years.'

'And it wasn't nice when they did it either.'

London zipped by outside the window, the houses becoming smaller and sparser as they headed west to Heathrow.

'It wasn't like we had a relationship. I mean, we kissed a bit, but we didn't sleep together.'

Ben coughed.

'What was that about? You're one to talk. When was the last time you went on a third date? Or even a second?'

It did surprise her that Ben was still single. He was successful, fun and smart. Not to mention kind. He was one of her favourite people in the whole world and she knew his single status was not due to a lack of interest or trying by the women of London. Ben was as allergic to long-term relationships as she was, yet no one ever seemed to pressure him to couple up. No one, but no one, ever seemed to worry that, at thirty, Ben was single. When he failed to commit, people said that was just what men did, whereas when Charlotte declined a long-term relationship, people wanted to know what was wrong. Ben was single, but everyone said he just hadn't found the right woman. Charlotte was single but it was because of a character flaw. Or worse, the tragic dark cloud of Tim's death.

The double standard was unfair.

He met lots of fabulous women. Her friends, for starters. She'd introduced him to a few in the hope they would hit it off, but nothing had ever stuck. The lack of suitable women wasn't the problem— London was awash with amazing single women who were successful, bright, and beautiful—and no one thought Ben's reluctance to buy someone a diamond ring and a house in a good school district was a problem to be fixed.

Further, Ben didn't have a reason to avoid commitment—something in his past that had scarred him for life. No. He was just a man and society did not put the same pressure on men to couple up.

Maybe his reluctance was due to his family. He was cagey about them and visibly tensed each time she brought them up. Now she'd finally have a chance to meet them and find out if they were the ogres that Ben believed them to be.

Charlotte contemplated this as the car weaved along the motorway.

She was quiet as they enjoyed their champagne in the lounge and as they boarded and settled into their seats.

'When did you last go on a date?' she finally asked.

'Why?'

'Just wondering.'

'Oh, I don't know. A few weeks ago.'

'Who with?'

'Julie.'

'Julie, the vet from Croydon?'

He nodded. She thought that had been months ago.

She studied Ben. Despite knowing him so well,

she still often got the feeling that he was holding something back.

Like his face, for starters. Ben had a jawline and it was sharp and strong.

And hot.

She fanned herself with her boarding pass as if she were some corseted lady who had never felt attracted to a handsome man before.

Which was ridiculous, because he was still Ben. The same Ben she'd seen yesterday at the exhibition. Drinking champagne with him at the East End gallery she'd felt nothing but a gentle buzz from the bubbles. But now, on the plane, her face felt warm, her heart rate elevated. And her stomach jumpy.

You're about to fly to Bali...no wonder you're a little on edge.

'Did she break your heart?' she finally asked.

'Who?'

'Julie!'

Ben groaned. 'No, she didn't.'

'Then why won't you talk about it?'

'Because she wasn't that important.'

It suddenly bothered her in a way that it never had before. Why was Ben single?

He was certainly good-looking. His eyes were blue and quick. And when he really studied something, they were deep and soulful. His hair was wavy and a lighter shade of brown, his figure solid but still lean. She'd never liked his overly thick beard much, but it was her own preference, and it didn't seem to bother other women. Charlotte often noticed women walk past them and give Ben a second look. The women would also often give Charlotte a quick appraisal, followed by a fleeting glance of disappointment.

Without the beard and with a more flattering haircut, he was…handsome. He had been hiding something under his too-bushy beard after all—impressive bone structure and full lips.

So why was he single? It was one thing for her to be. Committing to someone was difficult after losing her childhood sweetheart and the love of her life. But Ben had no reason not to be settling down with any of the lovely women Charlotte introduced him to.

Was he a bad lover? Was that it? Was he a horrible boyfriend? Unlikely. He was a good friend and, besides, as far as she could tell he was usually the one who was reluctant to take things forward.

The last time she'd set him up had been with her friend Kitty. They'd gone out twice, so twice his usual amount. But when a third date had failed to eventuate, she'd questioned them both.

Kitty had said Ben's heart was not for the winning, which was strange because Ben wasn't in love with anyone.

Ben had just told her that it wouldn't have worked.

But why?

What was Ben's problem?

She'd liked him the first moment they'd met. Not only was he easy to talk to, but they had lots to talk about. She had fallen into a relaxed and comfortable conversation with him. In the beginning she'd thought of him as a prospective client and then, for once in her life, she had a man who was a friend, who wasn't interested in anything more than that. And she adored him for it.

Charlotte studied him over the rim of her champagne flute. Ben was looking out of the window at the runway and sketching something in the notebook that was never far from him. It was his way of thinking, working and relaxing all at once.

'You know my friend Kitty?'

He hummed agreement.

'She's getting married.'

'Oh,' he said, but didn't look up from his sketch.

'Why didn't it work out with you two?'

Ben looked at her and pulled a face. 'What?'

'You went out a few times.'

'Yeah, but—'

The pilot came on the speaker to announce their departure just then, and Ben used the opportunity to avoid explaining.

Charlotte lay next to him in the flat bed on the long leg from London to Singapore, an eye mask covering her eyes, her dark hair half across her face, her chest gently rising and falling. They'd enjoyed a few more glasses of wine and dinner before Charlotte had done the sensible thing and changed into her pyjamas for sleep. She'd fallen asleep with ease, but now he nursed a Scotch and watched her.

He should get some sleep to minimise the inevitable jet lag on arrival, but his mind whirled.

He'd tried to make things work with Kitty; she was lovely, attractive, clever. But when he'd suggested they go back to his apartment for a coffee Kitty had crossed her arms and asked him what exactly he was playing at. Confused, he'd told her upfront that coffee really meant more wine, some kissing and perhaps something else. Kitty had told him outright that there was no point them dating when he was so clearly in love with Charlotte. He'd told her in no uncertain terms that he was definitely not in love with Charlotte. In fact, he'd spent ten minutes telling her all the reasons he was utterly, comprehensibly, and completely not in love with Charlotte, at which point Kitty had laughed, picked up her bag and strolled out of the restaurant.

But that had been three years ago, and he hadn't thought about it for two years and fifty-one weeks. He was glad Kitty was getting married, but didn't know why Charlotte was in such a snip about it all of a sudden.

She was plotting something. It was the uncharacteristic silences and the unusual looks she was giving him.

He hoped it wasn't a mistake bringing her to Bali. He'd wanted her to be close, but he also didn't need further complications this week. And Charlotte, somehow, brought complications with her.

Watching his mother marry someone else, having to deal with Will, that was enough for one person in one week. Would Charlotte make it easier to get through it all, or would her presence make it harder?

The flight attendant came past with cold bottled water and chocolate bars. He offered some to Ben, who shook his head.

'And would your wife like some for when she wakes?'

Ben opened his mouth to contradict the man, but then thought, *He doesn't care. The status of our relationship is not remotely relevant to whether Charlotte wants chocolate.* Ben just smiled, nodded and took the offered treats.

It felt nice.

Charlotte had thought Ben was exaggerating about the heat in Bali; she'd been to Spain and she knew what hot weather was, or at least she'd thought she did. The heat in Indonesia was intense, and the air was almost solid with humidity, weighing down on her like a thick blanket. By the time the car came to pick them up, she was already drenched with moisture.

The car took them from the airport, across the marina and down to their ferry. Ben had his face turned to the window and was letting the air rush over him. He'd left his baggy sweater behind and was now wearing a simple white T-shirt. His decision to shed his hair and beard before arriving at the equator now seemed genius. She twisted her long hair back but lacked a band to tie it off her neck completely. She harrumphed.

She kept looking back to beardless Ben. It was still Ben, but also not, at the same time. For the first time ever she believed that Clark Kent could go unrecognised as Superman with his glasses disguise. How had she missed noticing this Ben? The thin white T-shirt he was wearing left her glimpses of his well-defined biceps and the soft brown hair covering his strong forearms, not to mention the dip at his throat, which displayed a hint of the top of his chest. Charlotte let out another harrumph and tried to blow air up her face to cool herself down. It had precisely no effect.

'Why did you grow the beard in the first place?' she asked.

He shrugged. 'Laziness?'

Ben wasn't lazy, though, he was driven and hard-working. He painted every day. If he couldn't paint, he sketched. And he sketched constantly, filling at least one sketchbook a week with drawing and thoughts. The man rarely stopped moving.

'I don't believe that,' she said and he laughed.

Even his laugh was different without the beard. She could see his smile properly, the lines around his lips. The dimple.

Ben had a dimple, she saw now. Just one, a gorgeous little dent to the right of his lips. She wanted to reach over and press a fingertip to it, but stopped herself just in time.

'Was it to hide your dimple?'

He looked horrified. 'My what?'

'Dimple. Just there.' She pointed to it. Her finger stopped just millimetres from his skin, but he flinched and she snatched her hand away.

It wasn't just the dimple she wanted to feel, it was his bare cheek. She wanted to run a finger down it, see if it felt as smooth as it looked. She also wanted, she realised with a further blush, to touch the ends of his unruly curls that bounced in a way his longer hair never had.

Oh, the heat was more discombobulating than she'd expected.

'When I first moved from Adelaide, it was easier. Cheaper. I wasn't flush with funds and I spent what little money I did have on paint and instant noodles. Not razors. And then I found I liked it. I looked older. People treated me more seriously. Investors expect artists to be bohemian. Not conservative.'

The look he was wearing now was hardly conservative. Sure, it wasn't the full beard and long locks he'd had two days ago, but it wasn't a short back and sides either. His thick brown curls went in all directions from the crown of his head, messy and untamed and licked at the nape of his neck. He still looked slightly unkempt. Ruffled. As though he'd just climbed out of bed.

And it suited him.

Charlotte's mouth felt parched at the thought. She searched her bag for a water bottle to sip. Couldn't find one.

'But you stuck with the beard, even when you could afford a razor?'

'Would you like to shave your face every day?' She shook her head.

'It's freaking you out a bit, isn't it?' He held her gaze and her stomach did a strange floppy thing it never usually did when Ben looked at her. She looked away.

'No! Okay, I'm surprised, but it's not freaking me out, I just need time to get used to it.'

'You hate it, don't you?' he asked again.

She considered her answer. She didn't hate it, it really suited him. But he didn't look like the Ben she knew.

Which was ridiculous, because she did know him. Very well. She'd spent hours and hours in his company, talking, laughing.

Now, he looked like someone she'd swipe right for.

She would have to get past these strange new feelings because he was her best friend. After her parents, he was probably the most important person in the world to her and she wasn't about to ruin that with a silly crush.

She sought his eyes out. They, at least, were familiar, unchanged by his trip to the barber. She looked deep into them, blue and bright. Only now she saw that they were the same brilliant blue as the water the ferry was cutting across. With flecks of emerald the same colour as the lush greenery that seemed to cling to every spare surface on the island.

Locking gazes with hers, his irises suddenly opened with a flash, wide and seemingly large enough to look into her soul and read her mind.

Ben's eyes are gorgeous.

Oh, no.

That was not a thought she wanted him to read.

She looked down. Had his eyes always looked like this or had the Bali sun transformed them, brightening the blues and bringing out the occasional shards of tropical green?

What was going on with her?

'You do hate it. It's okay, you can say.'

'No, I don't hate it at all,' she said honestly. If

it hadn't already been so hot, her face would have felt warm. 'I'm just getting used to it.'

That was all. By tomorrow, he'd be just Ben again. And her stomach would have stopped being so damned flippy. Her body temperature would be back under control.

It was a half-hour ferry ride over to the island they were staying on, Nusa Lembongan, just off the coast of Bali. They were greeted by a man in a small truck, who took their bags. He pointed to the bench seat and motioned for them to climb in.

Charlotte eyed the truck and Ben explained, 'There are no cars on the island, just some of these small trucks for transporting goods or tourists to their hotels.'

'If there are no cars, how will we get around?'

'Walk. Motorbike. Cycle.'

Charlotte flinched. She didn't cycle. She certainly didn't motorcycle. Not since Tim's accident.

'It's okay,' Ben said, sensing her fears. 'The villa is close to restaurants and cafes and everything else we need is certainly within walking distance.'

Ben was right, the truck only drove them a short distance from the ferry dock, up a low hill to their accommodation. They passed through a village, which was filled with numerous cafes and food stalls, and her worries about having to cycle her way around the island abated.

They were dropped off at a group of villas that Ben's mother had booked for the wedding guests. Walking into their villa was like stepping into a celebrity's Instagram feed.

Her room had a high wooden ceiling, like a tropical hut. The walls were made of glass and slid open to give the effect of the entire room being open to the ocean, which glistened vivid aqua blue below.

Just like Ben's eyes.

She closed her eyes and shook the thought away. She just needed a proper night's sleep. Once she had adjusted to the time zone…

Charlotte pushed open another door and found herself standing next to an infinity pool and across the pool Ben stood in his room, also staring, slack jawed, at the view.

'Oh, wow…' She exhaled.

Purple flowers climbed up the walls, a small table was laid out with a water jug, dripping with condensation, and next to it was a bowl of tropical fruit. For eating or decoration, Charlotte wasn't sure.

She stepped out of her room and onto the deck that adjoined both their rooms. 'This is amazing. Can we move here?'

'Sure.'

'You're joking, but I'm not,' she replied. 'I think you're going to have to pick me up and carry me home. I don't ever want to leave this place.'

'You might change your mind when you meet my family.' His jaw tightened and she could almost hear the sound of his teeth clenching, enamel on enamel.

It was strange, being able to see the muscles in Ben's face and neck react in a way she hadn't before. What else had she missed about him? What else had she failed to see in the man who was supposed to be her closest friend?

She shook her head. 'Unless they're serial killers, this place is still worth it.'

There was a knock at the door.

'Speaking of which.'

'Who is it?'

'I'm guessing it's the family.'

Ben drew a resigned breath and she wanted to reach over and squeeze his arm, but he turned and moved towards the door before she could.

Charlotte heard a middle-aged Australian woman cry, 'Benji, sweetheart, I'm so glad you're here.'

Benji. She smirked. She was never going to let him forget that. She took a big breath and pressed her hand against her stomach, which was suddenly jumping with nerves, though she wasn't sure why. She wasn't worried, she was just curious to finally meet Ben's mother.

Charlotte moved to the living room of the villa. Ben's mother held him in a tight hug, then pulled back so she could look at him properly.

'Oh, thank goodness you've shaved off that awful beard,' she said, and patted his face.

Charlotte stood by, shifting from foot to foot, feeling like an intruder watching the family reunion.

Diane clearly adored her son.

Ben turned and, spotting Charlotte, said, 'Mum, this is my friend Charlotte.'

Was it her imagination or did he stress the word 'friend'? As if there was no way she could ever be his *girl*friend.

Girlfriend.

The nerve-endings in her belly did another dance. This time a vigorous Charleston.

Before she could step forward, Diane let go of Ben and moved over to her.

'At last! The lovely Charlotte!' Diane held her hand out, and Charlotte lifted hers, expecting a shake, but Diane pulled her into a hug that smelled of Chanel N°5.

'I'm so glad to finally meet you.'

'Me too,' Charlotte replied into Diane's hair.

Diane was beautiful. It shouldn't have been a surprise—after all, Ben was not unattractive, especially since he'd lost his scraggly beard and cut his hair.

'Thank you so much for inviting me. And for this.' Charlotte spread her hands around.

'No, thank you. Thank you for coming and for bringing my prodigal son.'

Charlotte looked at the floor. Diane's comment was sincere; it was clear she knew Ben had taken some convincing to come.

'It's so beautiful.'

'Isn't it? I'm so happy here. Get changed and unpacked, then come and meet Gus. Will and Summer don't get here until tomorrow, so tonight it's just us.'

'Summer?' Ben asked.

'Yes, Will's girlfriend.'

'Will has a girlfriend? Will Watson?'

His mother swatted the air. 'Oh, don't be ridiculous. You know Summer, they've been together for years.'

Charlotte got the impression that Ben most definitely did not know Summer. The two brothers were more estranged than she had realised.

CHAPTER THREE

CHARLOTTE WAS RELIEVED to take off her London clothes and have a refreshing shower following the flight. She chose a light white cotton dress for dinner, and, once dressed, studied herself in the mirror. Her hair had doubled in size in the humidity, and she was unaccustomed to the volume. She tied it into a loose braid to keep it off her face and slipped on a pair of sandals.

She walked to the living area and found Ben waiting. He'd showered and changed as well, into blue shorts and a loose white shirt.

Ben in shorts.

His legs were more tanned than a Londoner's had a right to be in October, as if he couldn't quite shake his Australianness, even after all those years. The top few buttons of his shirt were also undone, giving her a view of much more of Ben's skin than she was accustomed to.

Not that it mattered. It was no big deal at all.

He must have read her thoughts because he

rubbed his chin. 'I know, I know. I'll grow it back after the wedding.'

She stepped up to him and said, 'No.' Then, without thinking to stop and wonder if her gesture would be inappropriate, she did what she'd wanted to do since he'd first picked her up all those hours ago outside her flat. She lifted her index finger and touched his cheek. It was no longer freshly shaven, and with a smattering of stubble it felt like a fine sandpaper—rough, but far from unpleasant. She dragged her fingertip across it to get the full effect.

'No,' she repeated. 'Don't.'

For the second time in as many hours they locked eyes. The crease between his eyes deepened and he narrowed his gaze with a wordless question.

He exhaled, but neither of them moved. Instead, they simply stood at the door, with her finger resting against his chin, for a moment too long.

Finally, Ben turned his head away. 'We'll be late,' he said, his voice ragged.

He coughed and they left.

The restaurant was a ten-minute walk away and it was invigorating to be out and about, seeing this beautiful but unfamiliar place. Over the water, back towards Bali, the sun was setting into one of the most magnificent sunsets she'd seen in her life. The entire sky was lit up in pinks, oranges, purples. Not for the first time since their arrival they both stopped, awestruck by the view in front of them.

'I thought I knew what a sunset was. I was wrong. Have you seen a sunset like this?'

'Never. I want to paint it.'

She smiled. That was so Ben.

His work was his life. That was probably why he didn't want to date poor Julie. Or Kitty. Or any of Charlotte's friends. He was just too focused on his career. The answer to the question she'd been asking herself since London was as simple as that.

As well as the lack of facial hair, there was something else different about Ben tonight. And it wasn't as pleasant.

He was anxious. Stretched tighter than a new canvas, ready to tear.

For once, she had the strange sensation of feeling as if he was relying on her to be the strong one, rather than the other way around. She needed to be calm for him.

In London he was a self-contained unit. Strong, always emotionally stable. Here she saw a quality in him she hadn't noticed before. Hesitation. Uncertainty.

Vulnerability.

When they reached the door to the restaurant, he stopped.

Ben was about to meet his new stepfather. The man that would marry his mother in less than a week. It was enough to make anyone pause.

She took his hand and squeezed it. It wasn't a gesture she made often but tonight demanded it. She wanted him to know she was there for him, as he'd always been there for her.

'We can turn around and go back, if you like?' She knew he wouldn't agree, but she wanted him to know it was an option.

'She's marrying this guy. What if he's awful?'

'Why would you think that?'

Ben didn't answer.

Because his father had been. Because his father had been difficult and overbearing and what if Diane had chosen another man just like him?

'If he's awful, we'll leave.'

'We can't do that.'

'No, you're right. But if he's really awful we'll just drink more. And we'll have more to talk about later.'

A smile crept over his lips.

'If he's nice, we'll have nothing to make fun of.'

He squeezed her hand but didn't let it go. She squeezed back and they entered.

Charlotte was more curious to meet Gus than she wanted to admit. Ben was nervous, but that didn't mean that she had to be. She was an objective bystander. Besides, she intended to get to the bottom of the surprising relationship between Gus and Diane. She was less intrigued by the age gap and more about why Diane had decided to remarry so soon after the death of her husband. Would Gus be a sleaze preying on a vulnerable woman? Or a gold-digger?

They were both about to find out.

Diane and her partner were standing by the bamboo bar when Charlotte and Ben entered, but they noticed them straight away.

Gus was good-looking and appeared more mature than his forty-seven years, with salt-and-pepper hair and a healthy tan.

He smiled broadly and confidently when he saw them enter. He used both of his hands to shake Ben's and kissed Charlotte on both cheeks.

Their table was on the deck, overlooking the water, and the brilliant sunset provided the backdrop.

'Gus knows this place well. Are you happy for him to order for us?' Diane asked.

'Do you like your food spicy?' Gus asked them both.

They nodded, but with trepidation. Everyone's definition of spicy differed. Gus ordered, speaking Indonesian.

'Most locals speak Balinese,' Diane whispered, 'but many speak Bahasa Indonesian and English too. Gus just spoke Bahasa.' There was a hint of pride in her voice.

Gus and the waiter shared a joke that no one else understood. He seemed to be on good terms with the staff.

The food was delicious and thankfully the waiters kept bringing cold beers. Charlotte preferred wine but Gus assured her that with spicy food beer was the best option. He wasn't wrong.

Plates of satay and rice weighed down the table and her mouth watered. The food was delicious and Gus was proving to be a good host. A positive tick in Charlotte's list.

With Ben clearly finding the situation strange, Charlotte felt overly obliged to help carry the conversation. It was one of the reasons she'd come, after all, to be the lubricant and peacemaker in these awkward meetings.

But making conversation with Diane and Gus wasn't an effort at all.

Gus was ready to talk and, as part of her mission to subtly find out whether he was good enough for Diane, she quizzed him. He had lived an interesting life: he'd made a small fortune by the time he was thirty developing several computer programs in the tech boom at the turn of the millennium, but had then moved on to mentoring young entrepreneurs and had established a series of annual symposiums on all sorts of emerging technologies and ideas.

Gus was impressive, charming, and Charlotte could see why Diane had fallen for him. He was also mature and intelligent, and Charlotte could see why he'd be drawn to an older, but no less impressive woman, like Diane.

Gus was also making an extra effort to talk to Ben.

'I love your work, Ben.'

Charlotte felt Ben stiffen next to her.

'You do? Where have you seen it?'

'Will has one of your pieces in his office.'

'I don't think so,' Ben said.

'I'm sure of it. It's the ocean and a beach in the distance. From the point of view of a swimmer. It's so big.' Gus stretched out his hands.

Ben looked to Diane for confirmation, but she was suddenly busy beckoning the waiter. Charlotte didn't recall a painting of Ben's that would fit that description, but maybe it was one of his earlier works.

'Why choose Bali for the wedding?' Charlotte asked, changing the subject as it was obviously making Ben uncomfortable.

'We met here.'

Diane picked up Gus's hand. 'A year ago. At one of Gus's symposiums. I wanted to learn more about ocean waste management for our company, and Gus had organised a series of lectures on ocean conservation.'

Ocean waste management?

If you could be attracted to someone talking about that, it must be love, Charlotte thought.

'And it's one of the most beautiful places in the world, don't you think?' Gus asked Charlotte but he was looking at Diane.

'He does a lot of work for an NGO here. He won't tell you that, because he's too modest, but I'm allowed to,' Diane said.

Diane looked radiant. Her shiny grey hair was cut into a stylish bob and her skin was soft and fresh. The couple only had eyes for one another.

Watching them together over dinner, Charlotte had no doubts that Diane's feelings for Gus were real. And Gus clearly adored Diane and was not in need of her fortune.

Watching the pair of them made Charlotte believe that there was such a thing as soul mates. Two people so perfectly matched, two halves of the same soul.

She missed having that connection with someone, longed for it in her chest.

It was a concept she hadn't allowed herself to think about for years. Because if there was only one soul mate for everyone then hers had gone. Would it ever be possible to find someone else? Even if it was, did she want that?

She couldn't let herself get as close to someone as she'd been to Tim.

If she'd lost one soul mate, there was every chance she could lose another.

Charlotte was quiet as they walked back to their villa.

Or maybe she wasn't speaking because she knew he couldn't. The trip, the dinner, the whole day had left him tired in his bones. And then, to top it all off, there was that strange moment with Charlotte before dinner when she had stroked his face.

She'd slid her finger from his cheekbone to his chin and he'd felt every single one of the grooves in her fingerprint. Two hours and several beers later, he could still feel her touch like a burn.

He could tell his new look was throwing her; she looked at him as if he were a stranger. It hadn't been his intention to unsettle anyone. He had simply decided it was time for a change, something that would be more comfortable in the heat. There was something new in her eyes though. An intensity he'd never seen before.

Was it desire?

No. That couldn't be it. Charlotte was most definitely not attracted to him, and the absence of a beard wasn't going to change that.

Charlotte was not remotely superficial—just one look at the eccentric line-up of men she'd dated in the past few years proved that. The barrier between her and a committed relationship was much greater than just some facial hair. It was a dead boyfriend she wasn't over and an unshakable fear of falling for anyone else.

They walked the path through the lush undergrowth back to their villa. It rustled with unseen nocturnal animals.

'Are there snakes here?' she asked.

'Um… I'm not sure.'

She moved closer to him, and their shoulders bumped and for a moment her bare forearm brushed against his. At least in London when that happened one of them was likely to be wearing sleeves. Now her skin collided with his, soft and silky, strangely intimate.

He laughed to hide the fact that he'd really rather enjoyed the brief skin-to-skin contact. 'So it's okay for the python to attack me?'

'You're bigger. It'll take longer to wrap itself around you.'

As they reached the villa she said, 'So, we're safely out of earshot now. Tell me, what did you think of him?'

Ah, Gus. He'd managed to avoid that conversation for ten whole minutes. Ben's thoughts and feelings were colliding; he wasn't sure exactly what he thought. Even less about what he felt.

'He seems fine.'

'Fine. What a great review.'

'I just met him. That's all I've got. I'm happy for them, really.'

Gus did seem like a good guy, and Ben hadn't spotted any red flags—and he was certainly looking for them. Gus had only taken his eyes off Diane to respond to Charlotte's intense questioning. What did he do? Where did he grow up? What did he study? What were his hobbies? Favourite foods? Charlotte could have made Gus her mastermind topic after the evening was out, but

Ben was grateful to her for handling the cross-examination because Ben couldn't ask those questions of Gus without appearing to be mistrustful or disapproving. Coming from Charlotte the questions seemed like nothing more than natural curiosity.

Ben was no longer ambivalent about Charlotte's presence, he was downright grateful. She'd been the one to nudge him through the doorway of the restaurant and having her beside him all evening had made him feel calm and centred. She had talked about herself too, and her gallery. The conversation had flowed smoothly and naturally.

Meeting your mother's new fiancé wasn't necessarily one of the most stressful situations in a person's life—Ben had certainly been through worse—but it was still unsettling and he was grateful Charlotte had been there to hold his hand.

Quite literally.

Ben flexed his fingers now.

Holding hands at that moment had felt so natural he only now reflected on the fact that it wasn't something they usually did.

It had felt nice. He rubbed his hands together, shaking off the sensation. Holding hands wasn't something friends did. Even good friends as they were.

'Ben, really. It's okay, we can talk about it.'

Ben sighed. 'I don't have a problem with the marriage.'

'I know.'

Ben slipped the key card out of his pocket and unlocked the door to their villa. They stepped inside.

'I don't care that he's younger.'

'Good.'

'I don't care that he's good-looking.' He put the key card down on the table with a little too much force.

She laughed. 'Ben, it's okay.'

Charlotte reached over and wrapped her hand around his forearm. His skin prickled. He wanted her to rub his arm. He longed to feel the friction between their skin.

'It's okay to find this situation weird. It wouldn't matter who she was marrying, it's the fact it's happening so soon after your father's passing. You're allowed to be sad about your father. You're allowed to have mixed emotions.'

He looked down at her hand, warm against his forearm. She rubbed her thumb against the soft skin under his arm, probably just to reassure him, but sparks shot through him. It was an effort to focus on the conversation. What was going on between them? Bali was having a strange effect on them both.

With effort he brought his thoughts back to the conversation and away from wondering what it would feel like if he too lifted his hand and stroked her arm…

'I don't want her to think I'm not supportive.'

'She doesn't think that. She's just glad you're here. That you've come. I don't think she wants to upset you either.'

'Dad was difficult; he caused lots of tension in my life and I never truly felt that he loved me. So I am glad she's found someone.'

Charlotte nodded.

'And he seems like a good guy. But that's all I've got.'

It was the truth. Jet lag, dinner and the beers were all catching up with him. There was an un-easiness inside him he couldn't place, but he knew it likely had to do with the woman in front of him. Stroking his arm with her soft thumb.

But now was not the time to try and analyse it.

Charlotte let go of his arm but leaned in and wrapped him into a hug. He leaned into it. He could ponder later on what was going on in Char-lotte's mind. Right now, he was grateful for the touch, the support. Her warmth.

'Thank you for being here,' he said into her hair. She still smelt of London, of her shampoo. Of roses.

'I wouldn't have missed it.'

When they pulled apart, she stood on her toes and lifted her face to his.

'Goodnight,' she said, and kissed him. It was meant to be on the cheek, he was sure, but the kiss landed half on his cheek and partly on his mouth. An accidental brush was all it was, but he had tasted her lips. The last of her lip gloss, the beer she'd had with dinner, the salt from the light sweat that skimmed her skin. He brushed his tongue over his bottom lip, tasting her again. She turned and walked to her room, leaving him standing there, watching her go, wondering for the umpteenth time that night: what was going on with Charlotte?

Charlotte woke some hours later, drenched with sweat and wide awake even though it was still dark outside. The last thing she remembered from the day before was accidentally almost kissing Ben on the lips before stumbling to her room and falling into bed.

Accidentally, almost.

The edge of her mouth had touched the edge of his, enough that the sensitive nerve endings on her lips had felt the softness of his. The memory made her lips tingle and she touched them with her fingertip.

The same fingertip that had also stroked Ben's smooth cheek the day before as well. It was just a beard! Why was its absence making such a difference in the way she looked at Ben?

Steamy Bali was doing strange things to her brain. She and Ben were not casual kissing or hugging friends. On regular days, if he dropped into the gallery or if she popped over to his place

for a meal, they'd greet one another with a wave.
Ben wasn't overly demonstrative, and she understood that; he was Australian, she was British,
neither nationality known for unrestrained shows
of emotion.

On the few occasions they had kissed casually on cheeks—birthdays, celebrations and the
like—it had been quick and his prickly beard had
always been in the way.

This time was different. For starters, his prickly
beard was gone, leaving only smooth, bare skin
and exposed soft lips.

It had clearly been a mistake, a misjudged
movement, a kiss on the cheek that had missed.
These things happened. They didn't mean anything. She knew, beyond doubt, that Ben had not
tried to kiss her.

Charlotte ran her tongue over her lips.

*But what would it be like to kiss him properly?
Not accidentally.*

She shook the thought away as soon as it came
to her.

Not Ben. She couldn't kiss *Ben.*

Ben was her friend, her rock. Her confidant.
The person who cooked her dinner when she
couldn't be bothered. The person who she could
call, day and night, in any emergency. The person she could speak to about almost anything.
Who would cheer her up when things inevitably
turned sour with Ben, if not Ben?

Her parents and girlfriends had long since stopped being useful counsellors in relation to relationships. They couldn't understand why she just couldn't settle down with someone already.

It's been seven years, they would say. *Surely you're over Tim by now.*

The last part was implied, rather than spoken aloud, but it always hung in the air any time she'd mention that a date hadn't gone well or that she'd ended a nascent relationship.

Ben didn't judge her for all the false starts. Never implied Charlotte's standards were too high, as everyone else had.

'I think they have a club,' Kitty had joked once. 'The three dates with Charlotte Reid club. They'd like to say it's exclusive, but it's not.' Her friends had fallen over themselves with laughter in the wine bar at that one. From then on Charlotte had reserved discussion about her dates for Ben only.

Ben understood: he knew she just hadn't found the right person.

Sometimes she felt that she was getting there. She'd meet a man and he'd seem lovely and kind and then she'd imagine what their future might look like and that was usually the point at which things would start to unravel. Occasionally she might wonder if he could be the type of man she'd like to see more of, and this was harder, as when she imagined herself falling for him she'd be gripped with a type of fear and Tim would intrude into her thoughts more than ever. Tim when they first met, but also Tim in the hospital. Because was this new man worth the heartache? Would he be worth the pain? Or the worry? Maybe it was just better to end things and move on instead. Easier. Simpler.

Charlotte threw off the single sheet that had covered her in the warm night and walked over to the window. The sky was still resolutely dark.

But it wasn't rainy, like London. Today would be a clear, bright day.

Unlike that day, a decade ago.

The details had taken for ever to emerge. First the phone call saying Tim had been in an accident, but not to worry. Then at the hospital, where the nurses had met her with solemn faces. Then finally, tense discussions with the doctors and Tim's parents.

Multiple fractures, internal bleeding. Long surgeries and ICU stays. Their initial fears gradually gave way to optimism, but then a roller coaster of emotions tossed her around physically and mentally. One day they might be planning rehabilitation, the next they were discussing nursing homes. Some days he was conscious and lucid, other days the pain was so much they kept him sedated.

Days turned to weeks and one day she was surprised to come out of the hospital and find that it was spring. And then he was gone. She still marvelled that even after all those months it was a shock when he passed. Marvelled at the fact that one moment he could be there, everyone discussing the next round of treatment and rehabilitation, and the next he was gone.

Charlotte dropped out of her teaching course, realising that, without Tim, she didn't want to lead the life that they had planned. And she looked back to her first love: art.

Life was too short to make conservative choices. Her dream job—the one she'd never believed she could do—was as a curator. Now, feeling strangely free and unburned by planning for a shared future with Tim, she dreamed even bigger—owning her own gallery.

She studied and she worked and she didn't stop to rest, living her life enough for two people.

With that thought, Charlotte decided to start her day. The clock on her phone showed five a.m. but her body clock was on a totally different time zone. And she was warm already. She decided to go for a swim.

Charlotte floated on her back, holding herself up with long lazy strokes and looking up at the sky, still dark blue but getting lighter. The strange, unfamiliar constellations were fading. This place was magical. Relaxing, sublime. Other-worldly. Something caught her eye, and she flipped upright. Ben stood on the patio rubbing his eyes.

'Sorry, I didn't mean to interrupt,' he said.

'You're not interrupting anything. I'm just cooling down. I'm sorry if I woke you.'

Ben was wearing boxers and a black T-shirt. His pyjamas.

She'd never seen him in his pyjamas.

He's never seen you in a bikini.

Ben shifted from foot to foot and looked as if he was about to leave. This was silly. They'd be sharing a villa for a week; they'd have to get used to seeing one another with fewer clothes on. She swam over to the edge of the pool and lifted herself out. She turned her body and sat on the edge, dangling her legs in the water. She patted the space next to her. He looked around, but then joined her by the pool.

She looked down at her bikini-clad body. Was that why he couldn't meet her eyes? He was always a gentleman, she reminded herself, but they were on the equator and the temperature hadn't dropped below twenty-five degrees since they'd arrived.

'I take it you didn't sleep well,' he said.

'I did at first, but once I woke, I couldn't get back to sleep. You?'

'Same. We should probably try and get out in the sun today, get our body clocks to adjust.'

'Sure, what's on the agenda?'

'We're meant to have dinner with my family this evening, but nothing before that. We could go to Ubud, check out the crafts.'

Ubud was a town in the hills on the main island of Bali, known for its art scene. She wanted to go, but, after travelling around the world yesterday, she also longed to get her bearings just where they were.

'I'm happy to stay on the island and just explore here,' she said.

'Let's do that. I'm still adjusting to the time zone and, honestly, this place is just beautiful.'

Their feet dangled in the water and the last of the moonlight danced over the surface of the pool. She kicked gently back and forth and watched the ripples on the surface.

Her gaze slid over to his legs, bare and also gently kicking the water.

Her eyes travelled up from his big feet to his knees, which were covered in a light smattering of hair and a few drops of water. Without her realising what she was doing, her gaze travelled higher, to his shorts. His hands covered his groin. It was a strange posture to adopt; her hands were planted on the tiles behind her, which was much more comfortable than the pose Ben was in.

Why would he…? Unless?

No. Ben didn't think of her like that. They'd spent thousands of hours together over the years and he'd never reacted to her like *that* before.

But you've never been sitting next to him dripping wet in a bikini before.

Since that awkward and accidental kiss goodnight she'd been hyper-aware of her lips. Even now. She pressed them together.

The look he gave her asked, *What's the matter?*

And she couldn't answer him. She couldn't lie and tell him that nothing was the matter, because there was no denying something wasn't right. But she didn't have the first idea how to put it into words.

Ben was sitting there with his hands protectively over his crotch and she was wondering what it would be like to kiss him. That was what was going on.

But why? Were they different in Bali? Ben was sexy in Bali. There, she'd acknowledged it. Beardless Ben was sexy as hell.

She hadn't changed though. She hadn't shaved off a beard or transformed her appearance in any way, so why was he suddenly attracted to her?

It was the southern hemisphere and more than one thing was upside down.

'I think they'll deliver us breakfast soon,' he said.

'Yes, that's what they said.'

This conversation couldn't get any more prosaic.

'It looks like the weather will be nice today,' he said.

Wait, no, it could.

She turned to him, drew a deep breath and was about to say, 'What's going on?' when their gazes locked. She stared into the deep blue depths of his eyes, noticed the dark flecks that lay deep within. The sparks that danced across the surface.

She should look away; she didn't. Instead, her gaze dropped slightly lower, to his lips. Dusty pink, full. Her own tingled again.

He pressed his lips together, oh, so gently. Wetting them.

Before she realised what she was doing, she mirrored the gesture.

Oh.

Bali Ben was different. Bali Charlotte was too.

Slowly, as though testing the temperature of the water, she lifted her hand to his face. Instead of simply feeling the new smoothness of his skin, she placed her whole palm against his cheek. He didn't move. Didn't flinch, just kept his eyes on hers, let her lead the way. She splayed her fingers, discovered how his cheek felt against her palm. His eyes didn't waver, though his lids became heavier. She slid her fingers across his temple and into his now short hair. It was soft, smooth, just like his cheek.

It was ridiculous, touching him like this, and for a moment she wondered if in her jet-lagged state she was actually still asleep. The sky was now a lighter blue. The colour of Ben's eyes.

If you'd asked her a week ago what colour Ben's eyes were, she would have said blue-grey. Now they were the colour of a tropical lagoon. The Northern Lights. A magnificent opal.

This was madness.

She took her hand from his face but in a flash his hand rose and held hers in place.

Don't stop, said the eyes that were the colour of a Bali sky at sunrise.

He was still, almost as though he weren't breathing, and reflexively she held her breath too.

She was looking so closely into his eyes she felt she might fall into them, their mouths close enough for her to see each crease in his pink lips, each pore in his skin. His newly bare, smooth skin.

She dragged her hand down to his chin, tilted it slightly and leaned in. She closed her eyes but their mouths still found their way to one another's. Her lips pressed lightly on his, but neither of them moved further, each waiting a moment to see what the other would do. She parted her lips ever so slightly, enough to excite a spark of friction between them, setting off nerve cells through her body. Finally, his mouth opened and his tongue slid gently across hers. His kiss was slow and measured, yet still had the effect of igniting sparks through her body. He tasted faintly of mint, but otherwise the taste was new, unexpected. He tasted of Ben and she liked it. Needing more, she opened her mouth and fell completely, wholly, irretrievably into the kiss.

* * *

Ben collapsed into the kiss. It was everything. Like a guilty dream but so much more because this wasn't happening during an early morning REM cycle, he was fairly sure this was happening in real life. Charlotte was kissing him.

Out of nowhere.

Charlotte was kissing him. And no longer tentatively. Their mouths were wide open, tongues entangled. Her hands were wandering over his T-shirt, his down her bare shoulders.

He hadn't meant to react like that to the sight of Charlotte in the bikini, but it was morning and she was gorgeous, and he had some control over his body but not that much. His insides were slowly igniting, like a flame licking at paper, then catching on something more substantial.

But why? What had changed? The beard, maybe, but that couldn't be it. Or had it been him? Had his obvious physical reaction to her red bikini given too much away? No, it wasn't just the beard standing between him and Charlotte and a long and wonderful life together. It was much more than that. Because Charlotte wasn't ready. Charlotte wasn't over Tim. Charlotte dumped every man she dated after a few dates.

Charlotte did not mean to be doing this.

Once Ben's brain was in gear, his mouth froze. Charlotte's lips quickly copied his reaction. Their mouths remained touching, locked but unmoving. As if that would change anything. Finally, she pulled back.

'Um…' Ben muttered, forgetting every word he'd ever known.

'Yes—um… I'm sorry,' she said.

'Don't be,' he replied quickly. 'That was nice.'

Nice! Are you describing a cup of coffee? It was amazing. Life-changing.

'Actually, it was more than nice,' he added.

Charlotte looked down shyly, but he could see the smile on her face. 'It was, wasn't it?'

He needed to stay calm. He needed to make sure that whatever he said next didn't panic her and send her running. Then he looked down at Charlotte in her red bikini and God help him. He'd always been careful about not letting his eyes linger too long on her low necklines, knowing that it was a line he shouldn't cross, but no, in his current state of arousal, it took every drop of his self-control to drag his eyes back up to hers. It was even harder to find the right words to say next.

He had to take this slowly, carefully. As if he were holding the finest glass. He had to make sure she wouldn't freak out.

He put his hands back between his legs, covering his lap. He was trembling, the sensation of Charlotte's mouth on his still vibrating through him. He also had to make sure *he* didn't freak out.

'Ben?'

'Yes.'

He looked up from his lap and back to her. Her eyes were wide with concern.

He opened his mouth to ask her what was wrong but before the words were out her lips were back on his. Warm and wet and asking the only question he wanted to hear.

Yes was his answer. A thousand times, yes.

Her lips were silken and tender and she tasted like Charlotte. Like the scent that surrounded her, like the way his apartment smelt when she left it. But best of all, the kiss was like continuing the conversation they had started the day they first met. Natural, sharing, mutual. He slipped his fingers into her hair and she pressed herself against him. The world dropped away. This was his entire existence.

Breathless, they both pulled away, panting. She leaned against him and he held her as they caught their breaths.

'I'm sorry, again. I don't know what's come over me.' She ran her hands over her hair, her cheeks were flushed and her lips pleasingly plump.

'Don't apologise,' he said gruffly.

If only, instead of deciding that he would never kiss Charlotte, he'd happened to imagine what might happen if he ever did, he'd have had a plan for this moment and wouldn't be floundering now for the right words.

Because he wanted her. He wanted to kiss her again.

More importantly of all, he didn't want her to run.

A first kiss—their first kiss—wasn't the finish line; it was the beginning of the race. He was now simply lined up at the starting line with all the other men she'd dated.

He was just like Don and the rest, waiting for his Dear John text message. Or worse, waiting for her to hop and skip out of here and onto the next flight out of Denpasar. No. He wasn't going to be like Don or the other men because he knew her.

And that meant also knowing that Charlotte wasn't over Tim. And knowing, as he knew the back of his own hand, that Charlotte was going to self-sabotage any new relationship because of it.

'You're my best friend. And I don't want that ever to change,' he said.

She looked down and nodded. 'Yes, that's right. Sensible.'

'Don't get me wrong, the kiss was great, but…'

'Yes, I know. Our friendship. I don't know what came over me.'

'So you're not going to freak out?' he asked, knowing that simply by saying that she might.

'I'm not freaking out.'

Not yet.

'I didn't mean… I know you're not.'

'And you shouldn't freak out either.'

'I'm completely calm.'

Charlotte laughed and picked up his hand. It was still shaking. 'No, you're not. If anyone's freaking out it's you.' She pressed his hand between both of hers.

Oh, God. Her hand was as steady as a surgeon's whereas he looked as if he had a tremor. He snatched it away and put it back in his lap to cover the other obvious giveaway about exactly what sort of physiological reactions were going on in his body.

There was a knock at the door and Ben jumped up to answer it. Whoever it was had impeccable timing and he would have to remember to thank them.

When he remembered his own name.

He smiled broadly at the man who was delivering them the breakfast of fresh fruits, bread and hot, steaming coffee, which Ben had ordered the night before.

Thank goodness he'd had the foresight to do that. Hopefully a large cup of caffeine would help him figure out what on earth to do and say next.

CHAPTER FOUR

CHARLOTTE'S KNEES TREMBLED as she stood and went to her room.

She noticed the plants, the white couch, the painting of the jungle on the wall. Everything seemed sharper. Brighter.

Ben. She'd kissed Ben.

She'd kissed her best friend. And it had been wonderful.

Until, that was, it had become weird and more than a little uncomfortable.

You're my best friend. And I don't want that ever to change.

That meant he didn't want it to happen again. The message was loud and clear. She'd kissed him, without warning and without thinking, and possibly jeopardised their entire relationship in the process. He'd taken it well—he'd even, she suspected, enjoyed the kiss—but that was as far as his feelings went.

She was such a fool.

In her room, Charlotte's hands shook as she took

off her wet bikini. They still shook as she turned on the shower.

They couldn't even blame alcohol; they'd both been sober.

Jet lag, that must be it. Though was that even a thing? Did people do crazy things just because they were a bit tired? They might forget where they put their keys. They didn't forget that one wasn't supposed to kiss one's best friend.

Maybe she'd just wanted to kiss Ben. Maybe it was as simple and true as that, she thought as she let the warm water wash over her.

No, that couldn't have been it, there was nothing simple about what had just happened. They'd known one another for years, spent countless hours in one another's company and she'd never felt like this before. No, it was something else. And she had better figure out what it was before it happened again.

You're my best friend and I don't want that ever to change.

Ben was sensible. She didn't want to ruin their friendship either. Ben was…well, he was her closest friend. He made her laugh. News—good or bad—wasn't real until she told Ben.

She didn't want anything to change either. Especially not over something as insignificant as an impulsive kiss.

Even a really, really good kiss.

* * *

Charlotte dressed for exploring, in denim shorts and a T-shirt. The sun was fully above the horizon by the time she emerged, hesitantly, from her room.

Breakfast had been laid out on the deck, including fresh coffee, which she jumped on as though her life depended on it, and the most magnificent fruit platter she'd ever seen. Ben was nowhere to be seen, leaving her to look at the view alone. The fruit didn't taste quite as good without him. And certainly not with the worry about the kiss looming over her.

Surely one wasn't meant to feel like this about a kiss. Excited. Turned on. Joyful. Those were the emotions a kiss should elicit.

Not worry and a feeling of impending doom.

Exploring. That was what they were going to do today. As if everything were completely normal and nothing had changed. As if the kiss had been an early morning dream, gone with the sunlight. As if her heart weren't still racing.

But, she reasoned, they had to pretend that nothing had happened. If they could just get through today, put her reckless actions behind them, then they would be okay. They had to be okay. For the sake of their friendship.

She waited what seemed like an age for Ben to come out of his room. She was about to knock when his door finally opened, revealing Ben, who waved and smiled and looked as though it were any other day.

'Shall we?' He pointed to the door.

She nodded. He was wearing a pair of shorts that came to above his knee and a slim-fitting blue T-shirt.

To match his eyes.

Oh, Charlotte, really? This is Ben, not some guy you met on the apps.

She had to stop ogling him.

She certainly had to stop thinking about the kiss. With that thought her finger flew to her tingling lips and touched them. Just as it did, Ben turned to look at her.

Caught.

He was going to think she was obsessed with him, and he wouldn't be too far wrong.

They left their villa and wandered down the coast. With every corner the view changed, from beautiful beaches to a village, to rugged limestone cliffs.

Nusa Lembongan was surprisingly hilly, and they made their way slowly up to one of the villages and explored a local food market and a Hindu temple, but, despite the new and interesting sights and the beautiful stone temple, their conversation was stilted and forced.

'It's magical.'

'Yes. Really pretty.'

Last week in London they had used words such

as 'prepossessing', 'exquisite' and 'beguiling'. Now the best she could come up with was 'pretty'?

You can't push things, she told herself.

Something unusual had happened this morning, but things between them would get back to normal. They just needed to give it time.

They needed an activity, something to distract them both. As they emerged from the temple and put their shoes back on, they were approached by a young boy who handed her a pamphlet. Kayaking in the mangrove swamp. That was an activity! Something new they could try that would distract them both from the kiss.

Charlotte passed Ben the pamphlet.

'You want to go kayaking?' he asked.

'Maybe. I don't know. I never have.'

'Then let's learn.'

A driver took them the short drive to the north tip of the island and the mangroves, a dense forest of trees and a river that spread in a maze out to the sea.

They were shown to their two-person kayak, lying on the beach beside two paddles.

'Push it into the water and then climb in,' the guide said.

Charlotte slipped off her shoes and Ben pushed the kayak into the shallow water. It wasn't long before she realised the flaw in her magnificent plan to distract themselves—how was she meant to get into the damned thing? She lifted one leg very awkwardly over the side and tried to sit, but the kayak tipped.

She stumbled and Ben had to reach out for her to prevent her from ending up bottom-first in the water. He caught her with one strong arm and held her effortlessly. Her heart hit her throat. Instead of thinking about getting into the kayak she only wanted to slide her arms around him and pull him even closer. Strong, steady. Her Ben.

'Okay?' he asked, his hand still holding her and his blue eyes staring into hers.

She could only nod in reply.

'I'll go first,' he said.

Unlike her, Ben climbed in deftly, his muscular legs supporting his graceful movement into the kayak.

His shorts rode up and she could see the muscles defining Ben's strong legs. One more thing he'd been hiding under his heavily clothed London persona.

Ben held the kayak steady with an oar and Charlotte attempted her mount again.

She fell into the kayak with a thump, sending water sloshing over the sides, but thankfully without either of them ending up in the water. Her face burned. One more embarrassing thing to add to today's tally.

Ben manoeuvred the kayak in strong deft strokes, whereas Charlotte's oar hit the water awkwardly more often than not. She probably would have done a much better job if she hadn't been so distracted by the sight of the muscles in Ben's arms flexing and extending as he paddled. Her gaze travelled from the ripples under his T-shirt, past his firm biceps down to the veins in his forearm and hands.

Ben was different in the warm sun of the Java Sea. Half dressed, to be sure, but glowing in the sun. He was strong and capable; showcasing skills she'd never noticed in cold grey London behind a paintbrush or in an art gallery.

Physical.

The word made her mouth dry, even in close on one hundred per cent humidity.

If she wasn't looking at his arms, she was looking at his legs, his strong thighs.

Argh. She shook her head. She'd had way too much sun.

Charlotte tried to focus on what they were gliding past, the tangled roots, birds, and the occasional fish.

But the memory of the kiss floated just beneath the surface of their entire day together.

'It's cooler out here, don't you think?' Ben asked.

Is it? Charlotte wanted to reply. But she kept her mouth shut; the heat she was experiencing wasn't coming from the sky or the water, but the man in front of her in the kayak.

'Hey, are you just relaxing back there? Making me do all the work?'

Charlotte looked down at her hands. They were balancing a motionless oar.

She hadn't been paddling, she'd been concentrating so hard on not looking at Ben she'd forgotten even to row badly.

'Sorry, I was looking for the fish,' she lied.

Had he always had muscles? Did they always ripple when he moved? She was sure she would have noticed such a fine set of biceps before if he had.

To be fair, she didn't have many opportunities to see him do anything as physical as this in London. Sometimes he helped her move a large painting. Or held a door open for her, but hardly ever in a T-shirt. Never when his bare arms were exposed to the sun.

'Fish? Are there fish? Where?'

'Oh, I think I saw some before,' she lied again.

Normal. Everything was completely normal, Ben told himself as the guide dropped them back in the village after the kayaking trip.

They stopped for a late lunch before walking back to the villa. Charlotte had been jumpy earlier that morning but seemed calmer now they were sitting on a beach, eating spicy noodles they had bought from a street vendor.

Ben had grown up in Australia, had spent half his childhood at the beach, but the colour of the water here was like nothing he'd seen before. Fishing boats bobbed and the water sparkled.

A small group of people were standing on the beach pointing at something. When the crowd parted, they saw a pod of green turtles making their way slowly into the crystal-clear waters. A few younger, spritely turtles reached the water first, followed by a large, older lumbering one.

'Amazing,' she whispered.

Ben just nodded, captivated.

Even eating a meal together, something they had done countless times before, the conversation between them was limited. Whether it was due to the kiss or something else, he couldn't be sure, but he feared that the kiss had unsettled her completely.

Charlotte panicked at the first sign a relationship was going well.

And at the first sign it was going badly.

So he was stuck. The only thing he could do was to pretend that things were normal and hope that, with the passage of time, they soon would be.

He hadn't gone as far as telling her that they should forget about the kiss as that would insult the intelligence of both of them. Trying to forget was pointless, but agreeing to put it behind them and move on was sensible. At least they had both agreed that they didn't want their friendship to change.

He didn't have the first idea how he was going to navigate the next steps between them.

The first thing was that it shouldn't happen again.

Not because it wasn't good, but because it was *too* good. Kissing Charlotte was not something he trusted himself to give up easily, so he'd never kiss her again if that was the only way of keeping her in his life for ever. Losing her as a friend wasn't an option.

'What are you thinking?' she asked.

'I'm wondering what this colour blue is called.' It was a lie. The water was definitely cerulean but he had to say something that wasn't, 'I was thinking about that kiss we shared this morning, about your lips on mine and how they tasted of peaches and how, in all the years of knowing you, I've never let myself imagine what it would be like to kiss you because I was afraid it would be exactly like that.' There were so many things going through his head right now and almost none of them came under the heading of Things He Could Tell Charlotte.

'Always the artist.'

'The whole place is stunning.'

'Yes, it's so relaxing.'

He looked at her. She thought it was relaxing? It might have been relaxing were it not for the excruciating tension between them.

He'd been so grateful when she'd picked up the

kayaking pamphlet, as it gave them something to do. As soon as he got back to the cabin, he'd look up more ways to fill their empty schedule with activities—surfing, cooking classes, trips to Ubud—anything—he didn't care—as long as it kept them busy. And kept their lips far apart.

'I'm glad I came.' She turned to him and smiled.

Her smile felt like a hug and he smiled back. 'I'm glad you did too.'

'I'm so glad to be away from London. I should have been doing this every year. It's so much better to be somewhere else on Tim's anniversary.'

The feeling of pleasure evaporated instantly. It felt as if an elephant had just sat on his chest. An elephant named Tim.

'Well, next year let's go somewhere else, even if my mother isn't getting married,' he said, his mouth dry.

She picked up his hand and squeezed it. 'Thank you for understanding, Ben.'

And just like that, they were friends again. Just friends. This was her way of telling him that the kiss didn't mean anything. That it was just some crazy early morning blip. That was better than her leaving, but he still felt disappointed.

'I know you miss him.' Her hand was still in his and he allowed his thumb to glide just once over the soft skin on the back of it. 'I know this time of year is hard for you, so I'm glad you came too.'

'Yes, but it's strange. It's been so long. I'm not sure if I miss him or the idea of him.'

It was a strange thing to say. 'Charlotte, I know you date. I know you see men. But I also know that you tend to end those relationships before they even get going.'

'I just haven't met the right person, that's all.'

'Have you ever considered that maybe you're not over Tim?'

'I don't think I'll ever be over Tim. But I promised him I'd find someone else.'

Her words flicked something in his chest and his next words came out without thought or planning. 'But how will that be fair to the guy you choose?'

'What do you mean?'

'He'll always be second best to Tim.'

Charlotte stood and brushed invisible crumbs from herself and gathered her things.

'Well, then it's a good thing I haven't committed to anyone else,' she said primly.

He was on dangerous ground, that was clear, but, like a fool, he stumbled forward into unknown and possibly hostile territory. 'I know that you promised him you'd find someone else, but you aren't going to be able to have a new relationship until you're over Tim.'

She shook her head. 'It isn't that. It's just that I haven't found someone who makes me feel the same way.'

Something collapsed inside him. It was as if she'd punched him, but she was standing two metres away. Why would those words hurt him so much?

'I've never met anyone who gives me that same feeling. Of being swept away. Of violins, fireworks and grand gestures.'

Despite his best effort, Ben laughed. 'Real love's not like that. It's not violins and fireworks.'

Charlotte's face fell and Ben wished his words back.

'What do you know about love?' Charlotte crossed her arms. 'Well, what?'

She was right. What did he know about love? His relationship history was more barren than hers.

He pulled himself up and shrugged. It was the best he could do.

'Tell me,' she prompted again.

He shook his head. Despite being no more an expert in romantic love than Charlotte, he wasn't about to tell her what he thought true love was.

'Please don't lecture me on love when you can't even tell me the last time you were in love.'

'No, Charlotte. I wasn't—'

'Tell me what you think love is,' she insisted.

Standing there, with the sun bouncing off the water and straight into Charlotte's dark eyes, with the warm Bali air swirling around them, he looked at her, took a deep breath and gave it his best.

'Love is small, perfect moments. It's waiting. It's patience. It's being there, even when it hurts. It's forgiveness.'

He turned away and gulped. He had no idea where those words had come from. That that was even what he believed. What did he know about love? He had just picked a fight with his best friend over nothing. The person he cared about most in the world. He was in no position to lecture anyone about love after speaking to her like that. He turned back to apologise to Charlotte, just in time to see her brush a tear from her eye.

'Char, I'm so sorry.'

She waved his apology away.

'No, really, I am. I had no right to speak to you like that.'

'It's fine, really. What did you say about forgiveness?' She smiled weakly.

He was as surprised by his words as Charlotte was. Maybe more so. Patience. Small things. Being there even when it hurt.

She was no longer expecting an answer to her question, but he still tried to answer it himself. The last time he'd had a relationship that had lasted more than a few weeks had been when he lived in New York. He and Maya had had an amicable break-up when he'd decided to leave for London. They still emailed occasionally, and she'd even extended him an invitation to her recent wedding. He liked Maya, but their break-up hadn't left either of them heartbroken.

Who, then?

Instinctively, he looked across at Charlotte. Her mouth was tight, her footfalls a little too hard.

They both knew that was as far as things would ever go, so there was no point in feeling anything else. Less point in taking out the feeling that was causing a tightness in his chest and a heaviness in his gut and examining it in the tropical sunlight.

Yes, he loved Charlotte. Of course he did. But he wasn't in love with her. If things were different, then he might think about whether their relationship could develop further. Whether he would want to kiss her again. And again.

But things were not different, so it didn't matter what he wanted.

They walked the rest of the way back to the villa in silence. It couldn't have taken more than ten minutes, but it felt like hours.

As soon as Ben swiped the key card, Charlotte said, 'I'm feeling a little wobbly. The jet lag is catching up with me so I'm going to take a nap.'

'Good idea,' he muttered. 'I think I'll join you.'

Charlotte's jaw dropped and he realised what he'd unintentionally implied.

'I mean, I'll have a nap as well. In my own bed. Not in yours. That's not what I meant.'

Ben knew his face was burning. Despite their

best efforts, the kiss hadn't just made things awkward between them.

It had made them excruciating.

Ben paced outside Charlotte's door. They were due to dinner in fifteen minutes, and she still hadn't come out of her room.

She's done a runner.

He calmed the pessimistic voice in his head. He knew she couldn't have gone anywhere as he'd been sitting in the living room all afternoon, waiting for her to wake up from her nap.

Far from spelling a new, wonderful phase in their relationship, the kiss had just made things between them strained. They needed to discuss it better than they had, but it would have been easier to walk a tightrope.

Discussing the kiss meant risking her saying that it was a mistake. It risked having her telling him something she hadn't earlier—that it must never happen again. All they had agreed was that they didn't want their friendship to change.

And what did that mean?

He knew they shouldn't take things further. One kiss, one mistake, could be forgotten. Could fade from memory. But as Charlotte napped and Ben brooded, other thoughts intruded.

Maybe they could kiss again? Things were already awkward between them, so maybe another kiss wouldn't make things worse. It might just let them know whether the one they had shared this morning was an outlier. A wonderful, miraculous exception. They could kiss again and find out if what they had this morning could be repeated without it hurting their friendship. Or was his head just addled with sunstroke?

Ben saw the doorknob turn and then looked away, so he could turn back towards her, pretending everything was normal and he hadn't been staring at her door willing it to open. 'Hey, it's nearly time for dinner,' he said as casually as he could manage.

She wore a pretty pink linen dress that skimmed her knees and her shoulders, revealing her long, bare arms. Smooth and lean. He resisted the urge to lift his fingertips to them and trace their silky length.

As they walked out of the door, Charlotte said, 'I'm looking forward to meeting the famous Will Watson.'

Ben clenched his jaw. His brother. Always the competition. And now he'd piqued Charlotte's interest. Great.

'What do you know about Summer?' Charlotte asked.

'Absolutely nothing.'

'You didn't meet her last year at the funeral?'

'I had no idea she existed until yesterday.'

'I thought they'd been together for years. Isn't that what your mother said?'

'He hasn't introduced her to the family before now. I've no idea why.'

'Hopefully we'll find out why tonight,' she said.

Or not, Ben thought.

Will's love life was his own business.

The sun had set and the moonlight reflected in the calm waters as they walked the short distance to the restaurant Diane and Gus had booked for dinner.

Charlotte seemed to be as touchy as ever after her nap. She knew he didn't like talking about Will, yet here she was probing Ben about his brother.

'Why don't you ask him?' she persisted.

'Ask him what?'

'About her? About Summer.'

'Why would I do that?'

'Because he's your brother.'

'We don't talk. Not like that.'

'Maybe you should.'

'Why?' Ben and Will had not been close for years. And there was no reason for them to start now.

'It might make you feel better,' she offered.

'I feel perfectly fine.' Ben's chest tightened.

She snorted.

'What was that about?'

'So you can dish out the amateur psychological advice but you can't take it?'

Ben stopped walking, closed his eyes and took

a deep breath to stop himself from saying the first thing that came to his mind: Stay out of my family business.

'I am fine. And happy.'

'Are you?'

Ben opened his eyes to see Charlotte standing right in front of him, hands on her hips and staring him down as though she were trying to bore a hole into his brain.

'Are you happy? Content? Is everything in your life completely and utterly perfect? Is there *nothing* in the world you wish for?'

He swallowed hard, burying the true answer deep down inside.

'I am perfectly happy and content with my life.'

She turned to leave but he still saw her roll her eyes.

By the time they'd reached the restaurant he was wound tighter than a spring.

There was nothing wrong with him. He was happy. Well, happy enough. He was content. His career was going well, he had good friends, including Charlotte. And no matter what the little voice at the back of his mind was saying, at least he and Charlotte were friends.

Thankfully, they soon reached the restaurant, and were shown through to a deck overlooking the water. The dinner was to welcome the wedding guests who had arrived that day, including

Gus's parents, Diane's sisters and, of course, Will and Summer.

His mother was standing with Will and a woman he assumed to be Summer. When Diane saw him and Charlotte walk in, she waved and called, leaving him no choice but to go over and greet them.

Will looked the same as always—impassive, serious. He held out his hand and the brothers shook. Briefly.

Introductions were made and Charlotte gave Will a huge smile and a kiss on each cheek. Ben's gut twisted.

Summer Bright looked just like her name; she had flowing auburn hair, a long colourful dress, and sandals on her feet. She wore pretty bracelets on her wrists that jangled when she also greeted Ben and Charlotte with a kiss on the cheeks.

'They're so pretty. Where did you get them?' Charlotte asked, pointing to Summer's jangling bracelets.

'Back in Adelaide, but I'm hoping to go shopping for similar things here. I hear they have fantastic markets in Ubud.'

'Yes!' Charlotte exclaimed. 'Ben and I were planning on going tomorrow or the next day. You guys should come with us.'

'That'd be wonderful,' Summer replied.

The women were instant friends and Diane beamed as she observed Charlotte and Summer chatting. Will glowered and seemed to want to pull Summer away.

Ben shook his head. His brother would always be a mystery to him. A mystery he had no desire to explore.

Will's betrayal had been nearly as bad as his father's. Sure, it hadn't been Will who had treated Ben any differently, but Will had benefited from their father's favour. He'd never defended Ben. Will had stood by, accepting his father's time, attention and money, while Ben was made to feel like an intruder in his own home. Everything the family did revolved around the business and Ben's decision not to be involved was treated with scorn and derision.

While Charlotte and Summer chatted about Bali and their trips over, Will and Ben stood in silence, not making eye contact with one another. It surprised Ben that Will had chosen a woman so unlike him. Summer seemed genuinely warm and friendly. The opposite of Will.

At every dinner party, there was a good end of the table where there was loud laughter and another end that was calmer, even boring. Ben found himself at the latter. He was seated next to his mother's older sister, his aunt Sarah, and Gus's mother. The two women didn't appear to require him for their friendly conversation about bushwalking and grandchildren. Charlotte was, unfortunately, at the fun end, seated between Will and one of Gus's handsome friends.

Ben did his best to make conversation with Gus's parents and his aunt, while also straining to hear what Will and Charlotte were saying. And burning up inside.

He and Charlotte never bickered like this. Never picked at one another's wounds. He supposed he should have expected her response after he'd questioned her about Tim this afternoon. He hadn't planned it, but then nothing was going to plan today. Any plans he had had taken a U-turn when she'd sat next to him by the pool in the string bikini.

He knew why he'd leaned in to kiss Charlotte; it turned out the line between his platonic feelings for Charlotte and his desire for her was as thin as the straps on Charlotte's red bikini. But what had made her lean into him?

The look of desire she'd given him this morning hadn't been in his imagination. It had been real enough to hit him over the back of his head and push him towards her too. It had been real enough to make him forget that this was *Charlotte*, who still loved Tim, who fled from any connection that got the slightest bit intense.

It had been morning, just before sunrise, and they hadn't been the slightest bit intoxicated.

Maybe she just wanted to kiss you too?

The thought was so preposterous he almost laughed aloud.

He and Charlotte together would be a disaster, both of them running from any potential relationship the moment it looked like becoming serious. If their friendship was to survive, they had to keep their hands off one another.

CHAPTER FIVE

CHARLOTTE WAS RELIEVED to be seated at the opposite end of the table from Ben.

Bloody Ben! She'd spent the morning feeling funny in her belly each time she looked at him and barely able to keep her hands off him, but now, after their lunchtime discussion? Now she couldn't stand to look at him.

Fancy telling her she wasn't over Tim! Implying that she wasn't being fair to any of the men she dated because she knew, deep down, she didn't want a relationship. And then, to top it all off, he had the nerve to tell her what love was!

Ben, whose relationship track record was even patchier than hers. Ben, who couldn't even tell her the last time he'd been in love.

She knew she still missed Tim, but she was ready to fall in love. She had been for ages. She just hadn't met someone who made her feel like Tim did, and what was the problem with that? She wanted swelling violins and fireworks, and she would wait until she found them, no matter what her parents said. And especially no matter what Ben said.

Bloody Ben.

She was still steaming.

Ben's brother Will was lovely and she was very much enjoying his company. Despite their different appearances, she could tell they were brothers. He was about the same height as Ben, maybe a little broader, and his hair was much darker. Near black, it was cut into a style even shorter than Ben's new cut.

She doubted Will had ever grown a beard. No, she doubted he would allow his face to grow it. He struck her as the type of person who issued orders expecting them to be obeyed. The stubble on Ben's face was already pushing through defiantly.

It was hard not to compare them, even though that was what Ben had been afraid of, that she would start comparing him to Will and that she would find Ben coming up short.

But she'd never do that; Ben was the original, Will just a slightly similar copy. Will was charming and good company, but he wasn't the same. She didn't feel as relaxed around him as she did with Ben. And she certainly didn't feel any of the multitude of emotions Ben had inspired in her today.

She could reassure Ben he was her favourite brother and always would be.

With a stab of guilt, she realised she shouldn't

have picked at Ben on the walk over, continuing their argument from lunchtime. She especially shouldn't have asked him if he was happy. It wasn't fair. She knew things with his family were tense and instead of helping him through tonight, she'd inflamed things.

She didn't know what had come over her today. Jet lag? Hormones? She had no idea. But something inside her was off kilter.

Despite Ben's protestations that all his father and brother cared about was money, she learned from Will that the family business had evolved over the years from plastic manufacturing into recycling soft plastics. Will's passion for it seemed to extend far beyond just making money; he had genuine concern for the environment and keeping the business profitable so it could stay operating and keep many materials out of the oceans and other ecosystems. He had built it into the major business of its kind in Australia. Charlotte doubted Ben knew about his brother's passion; if he did, he might understand his brother better.

She sighed. It wasn't her place to tell Ben to talk to his brother and try to mend things. That would likely make Ben even angrier.

After the first course Gus stood up and gave a short speech, thanking everyone for coming, and singling Ben and Charlotte out for travelling from London. After the speech there were hugs and people moved seats. Charlotte found herself sitting next to Diane.

Charlotte looked around at the restaurant, which had been decorated for the occasion with tropical flowers and tea lights. The ocean waves provided a calming backdrop.

'It's so beautiful here. Such a romantic location for a wedding.'

'I always wanted to get married on a beach.' Diane sighed.

'And Ben's father didn't want that?'

'God, no, David would have hated this.'

Charlotte's mouth dropped.

'It's okay, I was young when I married David and didn't have the courage to ask for what I wanted. We got married in a church because that's what our parents expected. That's what everyone expected. But now, it's my choice. And Gus's.'

Ben had told Charlotte about his overbearing parents; his father had been behind many of the decisions concerning Ben, but his mother had supported them. Charlotte wondered now how much Ben's mother agreed with everything her late husband had done, whether they had been the team Ben had always thought them to be, but she didn't say anything.

'I'm so glad he's here,' she told Charlotte. 'Thank you for persuading him to come.'

'Oh, I didn't,' Charlotte said reflexively. Then stopped. Ben had been prevaricating about whether he would come until Charlotte's offer. 'I gave him a nudge. But we're both glad we're here. Me especially. It's so nice to finally meet Ben's family.'

Diane picked up Charlotte's hand and it felt natural for her to squeeze it. 'You've been a good friend to him. I'm so grateful. I know he has other friends, but you're special.'

'Oh.' Charlotte felt her face grow red.

'It's hard living away from your family, even in another city, but on the other side of the world it can be especially lonely. We all need a person nearby. A person to call on in an emergency. It's such a comfort to me to know that he has you.'

'I have him too. Honestly, he's always there for me.' Charlotte spoke without thinking. The words were true. Ben was always there for her. No matter what she'd done or where she'd done it. Fixing things for her, coming to get her when she didn't feel safe on a date. Holding her hair off her face after that New Year's Eve party that got out of hand. Listening to her go on and on about her business and which artists she should be chasing and selling.

'He's my rock,' she said and suddenly felt tears welling in the back of her throat. She'd been callous to him on the way here this evening. More than that, by kissing him this morning she'd treated their relationship carelessly. She didn't want to do anything to ruin her friendship with him. She cared for him too much.

She didn't want to lose him from her life.

Diane didn't seem to notice the emotion that was welling up inside Charlotte as she continued. 'He never saw eye to eye with his father. They were always arguing about priorities. Never saw all the things they had in common. Their ambition, their drive. It broke my heart when Ben left.'

He left because he didn't have the support of his family, Charlotte wanted to say, but bit her tongue. He left because Will was given all sorts of support—financial and emotional—that was not given to Ben. Her desire to defend Ben was nearly overwhelming.

Her reaction surprised her. Parents should treat all of their children equally, not favour one over the other because of their career choice, she wanted to say. But for the sake of maintaining harmony, she kept the thought to herself.

'I knew he was immensely talented; I knew that he'd be able to support himself. And his father did too. But it hurt that he never visited.'

'Maybe he never felt as though he had your support,' Charlotte said, trying to keep her tone non-committal. She knew exactly how hurt Ben had been by his father's words and actions. Ben had not only been cut off financially, but his parents had not shown any interest in his work. Not in the same way they had followed and nurtured Will's career.

It was the differential treatment between the siblings that hurt him the most. But Ben had told her to keep out of his family business, so she stayed quiet.

It hurt her to know that they didn't think Ben was good enough. How must it make Ben feel?

Diane changed the subject deftly though and asked Charlotte about her gallery, and her parents. Charlotte began to relax as they talked about neutral topics, but then Diane said, 'I understand from Ben that you were engaged once.'

The nervousness returned to Charlotte's chest.

'Yes. We were young but we were planning on spending our lives together.'

'You never found anyone else?'

'I'm looking, but I just haven't found anyone who makes me feel like Tim did.'

Diane nodded. 'And Ben, he doesn't tell me much. Has he been seeing anyone?'

Charlotte felt unexpectedly sorry for Diane, who she now thought seemed to genuinely regret the near estrangement from her younger son.

'No, at least not that he tells me. He's quite cagey about that sort of thing. I have to drag every detail out of him. It's strange, because he lets me prattle on about all my dates.'

Diane's brow furrowed and she gave Charlotte a look she couldn't interpret.

When the first guests began to leave, Ben caught Charlotte's eye across the deck and smiled. Her heart swelled.

They would be okay. No matter what had passed between them that day, they would get through it.

He raised his eyebrows. *Do you want to leave?* they asked.

She nodded. She was exhausted and unsteady. She could blame it on the jet lag, or the cocktails she'd drunk at dinner, but it was more than that. Confusion, being muddled. Despite coming to the other side of the world, Tim still wasn't far from her thoughts. But this year was different from the others. Because it wasn't just Tim in her thoughts, it was Ben as well. Confusing, overwhelming, twisting, all-consuming.

Their friendship was important, but it was more than that—*Ben* was important. And she wanted him to know that.

The kiss this morning and the conversation with Diane had made her wonder for the first time what it would be like to lose him from her life, and she didn't like the way that thought made her feel. Not one bit.

They didn't talk much on the short walk back to their villa. Ben swiped the card and the front door opened with a click. He held it open for Charlotte and as she walked within a breath of him to enter, she couldn't help but inhale.

Ben. Even his scent was different here. Sandalwood and jasmine. The soap provided by the villa. On Ben it was transformed. She made a mental note to pack some in her suitcase for the trip home and to leave it at his flat.

They stood in the foyer. She should probably go to bed, but there was still so much unresolved between them.

The conversation she'd had with Diane had been surprising and a little heartbreaking. She needed to talk about what had happened that day. Needed to know that they would be okay.

'What did you think of Summer?' she began.

'She seems lovely. Not at all what I expected.'

'How's that?'

'She's not the sort of woman I expected Will to find. You met him. He's buttoned up. Uptight in the extreme.'

'I think he's just shy.'

Ben snorted. 'You're thinking of Mr Darcy. Will is no Mr Darcy. He's ruthless and focused entirely on the bottom line.'

'I don't know,' Charlotte said and grinned at Ben. 'I saw him checking out Summer's bottom line.'

Ben smiled reluctantly.

What now?

'Call it a night?' he asked.

She was tired, but she still wasn't ready to end this crazy day.

'I had a nice talk with your mother.'

'Oh?'

'It was illuminating.'

'What does that mean?'

'It means I think I learned more about you to-night than I have in ages.'

'Really?' He scoffed.

'I didn't realise how estranged you were. And I didn't realise how much your mother regrets what happened.'

He shook his head. 'Charlotte, I asked you to not get involved.'

But she was involved. Ben was her best friend and she cared deeply for him. She hated to see him hurting. And she hated to think of him as feeling alone.

It's such a comfort to me to know that he has you.

She stepped over to him and slid her arms around his waist. It felt good to hold him like this. She pressed her head into his chest and squeezed him tight. She had no intention other than reassuring him that everything was okay, but as she felt him against her, the long muscular lines of his body against hers, something inside her shifted.

Charlotte lifted her head to look at him, but didn't pull away from the embrace. Ben's brow furrowed. He didn't say anything, but he didn't tell her to let him go. Or stop. Which was good, because holding him felt natural.

She lifted her hand and ran her fingers down his cheek, still bare, but now slightly rough. She liked doing that too. Touching him. Ben needed to be touched. And held.

And kissed.

She wanted to be the one to do that.

Ben still didn't talk, he was hardly moving, his frame still and hard against hers.

They'd kissed once without ruining things, hadn't they?

They could still be friends, but wouldn't this be better than being friends who didn't touch?

She wasn't sure any more about her fears from this morning. Friends could touch. Friends could hold. Friends could kiss. Couldn't they?

She lifted herself onto her tiptoes to find out. Her lips found his and thankfully his didn't pull away. He didn't immediately kiss her back either, but slowly, persuasively Charlotte moved her lips against his, teased them open and then all at once his grip tightened, his mouth opened, wide and luscious and dragging her in. She went willingly, gratefully. Their mouths danced and then tangled together. Wet and warm. Her heart swooped and her insides tightened with mounting lust.

Ben slid his hands into her hair and gently angled her face to fit her lips perfectly against his.

She felt her knees weaken and her inhibitions dissolve.

This morning hadn't been an aberration. Ben could kiss. *They* could kiss. They kissed so well together it would be a shame—practically a travesty—not to keep kissing.

Suddenly Ben pulled back. His blue eyes the

colour of midnight. 'What's going on, Charlotte?' His voice was hoarse. Strangled.

'I don't know.' And that was the honest truth. If it had been any other man, she would have answered, 'Just fooling around.' But with Ben it was more complicated than that. Even though they were friends, couldn't they just see what happened and where it took them? 'Do we have to know?'

'No, we don't. We don't have to name it. But...' He rubbed his chin. She really liked beardless Ben, she really liked that she could see his lips properly. Liked that she could see his smile.

What she *didn't* like was Ben's hesitation. Didn't like the way he kept pulling away. He seemed to be into the kiss, he seemed to enjoy holding her. Wrapped tightly in his arms as she was, she could tell how much he was enjoying it, yet he kept pulling back.

'But?' Her voice was small.

'But I want you to be sure.'

She stepped back, untangling her arms from his.

I am sure, a voice inside her head said.

'I think we should both be sure,' Ben added.

That was it, Ben was not sure. Sensible Ben. He knew that every further caress was a risk. What would happen if they kept kissing and holding and touching and moved onto undressing...?

What then?

She was in no doubt sleeping with Ben would be quite amazing. The question of what came after was too big, too scary, too unanswerable. Ben was right, their friendship was far too important to jeopardise. Already things had changed, their easy camaraderie replaced with awkwardness. The simplicity of trust had been replaced with uncertainty.

Charlotte nodded, but her heart was falling. Yes. They should both be sure. Her desire to be held by Ben wasn't worth risking their friendship for.

She stepped back. Despite every muscle in her body wanting to keep moving forward. This new need she felt for Ben was so surprising, both in its unlikeliness and its force. For years she'd looked at him as Just Ben, then the guy had had a shave and suddenly he was causing her insides to do gymnastics. What was going on with her? He was right, they did need to step back and wait until they were both in a steadier frame of mind.

Ben coughed. 'Ubud tomorrow?'

She nodded, and turned towards her room, still pondering the mystery of what was going on between her and Ben. Hormones? No, no change there. Grief? Maybe, given it was getting close to the anniversary of Tim's accident.

Warm weather and fewer clothes. Was she that frivolous?

'Sleep well, Charlotte.'

Commitment-phobe Ben was taking it slowly. Of course he was. It was what he did. Just as she dumped each guy after a few dates, Ben took relationships at the speed of a two-hundred-year-old turtle.

How was he so sensible? She was burning inside. A second later she would have pushed him onto the couch and straddled him.

He wants to take things slowly and carefully because he doesn't feel the same way.

He'd looked so devastated after their kiss, his brow creased with worry. He did regret it. He knew this had changed their relationship. If he'd enjoyed the kiss, he wouldn't have looked as though he'd just lost a pet.

Charlotte threw herself onto her bed. Now it was her turn to feel devastated.

Because despite what Ben felt, she wanted more.

Ubud was a ferry ride back to the main island of Bali and then a taxi ride up into the hills. They met Summer and Will at the ferry wharf and the two women greeted one another with a kiss. Ben waved to Will and Will grunted back.

Great. It was going to be a long day.

'I don't know why we have to go with them,' Ben grumbled softly to Charlotte when they were seated next to one another on the ferry.

'Because I like Summer. And because it's weird if we don't.'

Ben liked Summer too, but didn't think it was strange not to go on a day trip with them. Though he had to concede that, with all the kissing he and Charlotte now apparently did, they should be hanging out with other people to try and dilute the tension between them.

But they should have chosen another couple to hang out with; Will brought tension with him. It surrounded him like an aura.

'I don't know what she sees in him,' Ben grumbled and was rewarded with an elbow to the ribs. Which had the unfortunate effect of placing Ben's body on even higher alert.

'Shh, he's your brother.'

'But he's so uptight. And she's so not.'

Summer turned and looked at them from two seats in front and smiled.

'Shh. She heard.'

'She can't have heard over the boat engine.'

The elbow Charlotte bumped into him was yet another reminder of the new physical nature of their relationship. They'd kissed again last night, and even though they had again told one another they didn't want to ruin their friendship, neither of them had come right out and said it mustn't happen again. He wasn't sure where that left them or how he felt about it. Terrified? Most definitely.

But also maybe a little excited.

He'd managed any attraction he might feel to Charlotte in the past by not getting physically close, but Bali seemed to be literally throwing them at one another. So far this morning they had brushed hands as they reached to pour the coffee, bumped into one another on their way out of the door and collided getting on the ferry. Each touch sent sparks through his body.

Now, on the ferry, they were sharing a seat that really was too small for two adults and their hips kept bumping, prompting warmth and feelings and making him sweat even more than the equatorial temperatures already were.

'It's so sticky here, isn't it? Do you think we'll ever get used to the humidity?' She fanned herself by pulling the neckline of her dress, showing him flashes of the cream of her chest and the swell of her breasts.

Despite the humidity she spoke of, his mouth was bone dry. 'I don't know.'

As much as he'd wanted to scoop Charlotte up and carry her to his room last night, as much as he'd wanted to lie with her all night, tasting and exploring one another's bodies, he knew it was possibly the worst thing he could do.

If they slept together, and it was anything other than anti-climactic, if she got the sense that he felt anything for her, she'd leave him for ever. And despite trying their entire relationship to hold his feelings back, he feared that sharing Charlotte's bed would bring those carefully suppressed emotions to the surface. He had no choice but to take things slowly. So slowly she would barely notice they were happening. Like grass growing. Or paint drying.

One day at a time.

One kiss at a time.

One claustrophobic ferry trip at a time.

Ubud was heaving with tourists and locals alike. He'd been looking forward to visiting what was called the cultural centre of Bali, but also missed the relative tranquillity of Nusa Lembongan.

The four of them found their way to the art market the guidebooks raved about. Ben tried not to think about what might or might not be going on between him and Charlotte while Summer and Will held hands and looked adoringly at one another. Something about Will and Summer's relationship worried him; he knew he and Will were no longer close to one another, but if Will had been dating Summer for years why hadn't he heard of her? Why hadn't she been at their father's funeral? Something wasn't quite right.

The market was crowded and more than once he lost sight of Charlotte's dark hair. When she drifted off in the opposite direction, pulled by the crowd, he reflexively reached out and grabbed her hand. She glanced at him briefly, then slid her fingers through his, entwining their hands. Their fingers stayed like that as they made their way across the market. There were amazing sights, sounds and smells, an absolute delight for the senses, but Ben couldn't tell you anything about that market in Ubud except how perfectly wonderful it felt to have Charlotte's hand in his.

He was nearly ready to succumb, and twirl her into his arms, but his resolve held.

He wasn't going to be another Charlotte statistic.

'This is the place I was telling you about,' Summer said to Charlotte when they neared the other side of the market. As soon as Summer turned, Ben dropped Charlotte's hand.

The small shop was full of jewellery and clothes and Ben and Will stood outside while the women went in.

'Summer seems lovely,' Ben said.

Will nodded.

Making conversation with his brother was like pulling teeth. Will wasn't his favourite person in the world, but Will hadn't personally wronged Ben. That had been his father, Ben reminded himself.

'She's not the sort of woman I imagined you with.'

'What's that supposed to mean?'

Ben took a step back. 'Nothing, really. I guess I imagined you with someone more corporate. But it's good really.'

Will's shoulders noticeably relaxed.

'Sorry, mate. It's just… Do you want to leave the women to it and get a beer?' Will said and Ben nodded.

'Mum doesn't approve of Summer?' Ben guessed as the brothers took a seat on the deck of a small bar overlooking the bustling street.

'She's bemused, like you, but she doesn't disapprove. She seems happy I'm dating someone.'

'And Dad?'

The air stilled at the mention of their father. The brothers had not spent long together at the time of the funeral. Ben's visit had been short and he'd spent most of the visit with his mother making the funeral arrangements. Will had claimed to be frantic attending to the implications to the business. Just as it had always been with their father, business had come first. Even when your father had just died, nothing and no one was more important than the business, Ben thought bitterly.

'Dad never met her.'

'Really? I thought you guys had been together for a while.'

'Yeah, well, you don't need to be a member of this family to know that Dad would not have approved.'

It was as though Ben was suddenly seeing his brother for the first time. Sure, Will shared their father's workaholic tendencies, but what if Will didn't want to run the business but never had the same courage that Ben did to leave?

Poor Will, not even being able to introduce his girlfriend to their father because he'd feared his disapproval. Ben wanted to shake his brother and remind him he was a grown man and did not need the approval of a tyrant, and a dead one at that. Instead, he said, 'I think she might be a good fit for you. I think she might be just the type of woman you need.'

'Yeah, well.'

A wave of sadness washed over Ben; he and Will had been so close as kids, swimming at the beach together, playing cricket in the backyard, or computer games. If you'd asked Ben at any point up until high school who his best friend was, he would have answered, without hesitation, 'Will.'

But when they were teens, it had changed. Will had been enthralled with their father and Ben had drifted slowly but surely away from them both. Making money didn't interest him in the same way it seemed to interest them. And then his father had made Will his favourite and Will had stood by while he was given everything and Ben nothing.

'And what about you and Charlotte?' Will asked, but when he looked at Ben, it felt as though his interest was genuine.

'We're good friends, have been for ages.'

Will raised a single eyebrow and his lips quirked into a grin. For a moment Ben caught a glimpse of his brother of old.

'It's complicated,' Ben clarified.

Will lifted his glass and touched it lightly to Ben's. 'Yeah, mate, it always is, isn't it?'

The four of them had lunch and explored Ubud. In the afternoon, at the peak of the day's heat, they reboarded the ferry back to Nusa Lembongan. On the return trip, the two women shared a seat and Ben and Will did as well.

Once they had said their goodbyes, Charlotte grilled him on the walk back to their own villa. 'Did you talk to Will?'

'I didn't have any choice, did I, given that you monopolised Summer all day?'

'She's great. She's fun and such a free spirit. Did you know she's a cabaret singer?'

'A what?'

'And she sings in tribute bands. And she busks.'

'Seriously?' Ben couldn't have been more surprised if Summer had been a painter, like himself. The Adelaide Watsons were allergic to anything artistic or anything whose economic value could not be easily determined.

'I've told them they just have to come and visit us in London.'

'Us?'

The word hung between them like a grenade that had been activated but not yet detonated.

'Us. Yes, you and me.'

Were they now an Us? And when had that happened? He wanted to ask, but was terrified about what would happen if the grenade went off.

There wasn't a single part of Charlotte that was not burning up by the time they got back to Nusa Lembongan from Ubud. She was drenched in sweat, her face was red, but most of all her insides were tight and hot. She'd just spent a whole day being next to Ben, pretending that everything was normal and wondering what on earth was happening between them.

First, they had been seated together on the narrow bench on the ferry, their arms bumping constantly. Next, they were squished together on the even narrower bus seat; their thighs pushed together, sticky with sweat. Then they were jostled along the street together. Finally, in the crowded market Ben had grabbed her hand so they didn't lose one another. The hand-holding was for practical purposes only but in those ten minutes she'd got to know what it would be like to always be holding Ben's hand. It felt strong, and protective, filing her with a sense of safety. She found herself wishing he'd keep doing it once they were back in London.

Which was silly because they both knew their way around London so there wouldn't be any need.

But still. It would be nice, she'd thought.

And not just hand-holding. But kissing too. She wanted to do more of that.

And more.

She wanted to see Ben, not just in his shorts, but without them. She wanted to get to know what was under his clothes as well as she knew the rest of him.

That thought made her hotter still.

What's the worst that could happen if we slept together? Charlotte had asked herself over and over on the day trip.

The sex might not be good, came the answer.

That was unlikely, given the kisses they had shared.

The sex might be great.

In which case that could be even worse. If the sex was great, she'd probably want to do it again and then what would that mean for their friendship?

And what if, amongst everything else, their friendship got lost?

Somehow, she didn't see that happening. A friendship with Ben would be strong enough to survive whatever happened.

If the sex is great and we wanted to keep doing it, would that mean we were in a relationship? Does Ben want a relationship with me? Do I want one with Ben?

Those were the questions that she simply didn't have the answers to. That was probably why Ben was being so cautious—he wasn't sure if he wanted a relationship with her. And he clearly wasn't as physically shaken by their kisses. He seemed calm, reserved, whereas, inside, she was a mess.

Ben was always so cagey about his relationships, even though in almost every other aspect he was open with her. She knew some deeply personal things about him, like how his father had favoured his older brother, how he'd always wondered why his father's love had been conditional, how he felt happiest when he was painting. But, despite sharing all this with her, Ben still kept most details of his romantic relationships from her.

He had told Charlotte all about his teenage crush, she'd even once met Maya, the girlfriend he had left in New York, but he'd said next to nothing about his most recent dates, apart from details that she now realised were superficial— who the woman had been, where they'd eaten or drunk. But never how he *felt*.

And that was the one important thing that eluded her now.

As they left Will and Summer and approached their villa, undiluted awkwardness simmered between them.

'What next?' Ben asked, as they walked to the door.

It was a good question, but Charlotte was no closer to figuring out what was going on between her and Ben.

'I just don't know, Ben. I'm really confused.'

'I mean, do you want dinner? A drink?'

Charlotte's face burned even hotter than it was already.

'I mean, confused because I don't know if we should eat in the villa or find somewhere else,' she added, trying to cover her slip.

He nodded, but the sly grin that came over his lips made her wonder if she really had convinced him.

'I think the villa. I think we should get something in. We've been out the last two nights.'

As friends, they could talk about most things. Especially meal plans. But as potential lovers? She didn't know the rules to that.

Potential lovers? She was getting way ahead of herself. She wasn't even sure that Ben wanted to kiss her again. Let alone sleep with her.

A memory from their kiss the night before came back to her, a low, soft groan coming from Ben's throat as he pulled back from their kiss. Ben did enjoy their kisses, that was apparent from his heavy-lidded eyes, the flush of his cheeks.

Friends with benefits sounded crass to Charlotte's ears. But they were friends and they could also sleep together. Would that be such a strange thing?

She already knew she liked Ben, loved his company. And if they were lovers as well, wouldn't that be perfect?

If you were friends who cared for one another

and slept together, what did that mean? Would it be really possible to keep things platonic? To keep the physical from the emotional?

All these years that was how she had managed her relationships because it was the emotion that was the problem, that was what led to heartbreak.

She'd managed with other men, but could she do the same with Ben? She already knew him and cared for him, so it wouldn't be like the others. Was that a good thing or a bad thing? She had no idea.

Exhausted, but wound tight, Charlotte flopped onto the couch.

'It's still so warm.'

'If only there were somewhere we could cool off,' he said with a laugh.

'You're right, we should have a swim.'

Yes, a swim would cool them both off. It would also do something about the butterflies that had been multiplying in her stomach all day, the sweat that clung to them both. She went to her room to get changed.

She'd brought a few swimming costumes, a black one-piece and the red bikini she'd worn the other morning. Charlotte's hand hovered over her suitcase for a long moment before she swallowed hard and chose the bikini.

Ben took his time changing. By the time he'd emerged from his room, Charlotte was already in the pool, floating on her back.

When Ben walked out and stood by the edge of the pool Charlotte's body stiffened, then began to slip under. She righted herself and stood.

Ben was wearing the briefest shorts she'd seen him in yet.

Best of all, he was shirtless.

In the four years of knowing Ben, she had never seen him without a shirt.

There was no reason why she should have, but she now felt slightly betrayed.

He'd been keeping something from her.

Sculpted and strong and perfectly proportioned pecs, just the perfect shade of caramel and with the slightest smattering of hair. Her gaze travelled lower to his stomach, flat and taut, and her fingers itched to slide over it.

Heaven help her.

Ben sat on the edge of the pool and lowered himself in before diving under the surface in one fluid movement and doing some lazy laps. The muscles in his back and arms rippled under his skin with each movement. As he turned at one end, he caught her eye.

He'd seen her watching! Though perving was more like it.

Charlotte dropped under the surface, her face burning.

To stop herself looking at Ben and his secret muscles she copied him and started silently swimming laps of the pool, determined not to stare. She glided through the water with purposeful strokes. Yes. This was better. Exercise would help take her mind off Ben's chest and the soft smattering of chest hair she now knew he possessed.

The problem was that by not looking at him, she accidentally swam straight into him.

They bounced back from one another, then stood, facing one another other, chest deep in the water. She curled her hands behind her back to stop herself from involuntarily reaching out. There was no end to her embarrassment. She was trying to stay cool and calm, but her attraction must be written across her face.

'Sorry,' she muttered.

'Charlotte, are you okay?' Ben tilted his head.

No. She wasn't. She was confused, but excited. Worried, but there was an inevitability to what she was about to do.

She stepped right up to him. The water swirled around their bodies and she reached for his bare shoulder. Golden and strong. She rubbed it with the soft pad of her thumb.

Ben turned and climbed out of the pool in a hurry, as if he were running away. But she wasn't going to have it. They had to talk about this.

'What's the matter?' she asked, following him.

'Nothing.'

'Then why are you getting out?'

'Because I've cooled off.'

Charlotte scrambled out of the pool. They were

going to talk about this, because for starters she wasn't going to be able to sleep tonight if they didn't and, for seconds, she thrummed with need. With want.

'Do you...not want to touch me?' she asked.

'Oh, Charlotte.'

He looked pained. As if she were offering him a root canal and not her body.

He doesn't want you. He knows this could all go very wrong.

Charlotte stepped back, at a loss of what to do.

Be honest. This is Ben. You can be honest.

'I'm sorry. I really am. I don't know what's come over me. Something's changed and I don't know what or why.'

If she couldn't be honest, then what was their friendship worth?

'I want you to hold me.'

Ben's face reddened.

'And sometimes I get the feeling that you might want to hold me too.'

Ben couldn't respond. He was torn between lying and disagreeing with her or pulling her into his arms and showing her how correct she was. So he stayed frozen to the spot. Slowly, hesitantly, Charlotte stepped towards him until she stood within a breath of him, and Ben was almost lost. He couldn't argue with her without lying: he wanted her with a ferocity that almost frightened him.

But he had to stop; he had to be sure that she was sure and that this was not a spur-of-the-moment idea she would regret with a new day.

What if, despite everything he thought, she was sure? What if she truly was ready to put Tim behind her and move on? What if he, Ben Watson, could buck the trend that was Charlotte's love life? His resolve, his plan was unravelling as quickly as he suspected her skimpy bikini top could.

'I want you. I want this,' she said, and his heart almost stopped. She took half a step forward and their wet skin met. Their hands remained at their sides but the exquisite swell of her breasts pushed gently against his. Her hip bone rested against his and he almost swayed with longing. He moved one bare foot between hers and their bodies were suddenly flush.

She wanted sex. He wanted sex. But sex wasn't as important as everything else.

'I can tell you want this too. At the very least I can tell you're interested.'

Charlotte shifted her leg between his. His lips might be able to lie, but his body couldn't, and it was apparent to anyone nearby that he was very, very interested in Charlotte and her wet, bikini-clad body that was currently wrapped around his almost naked one.

What was holding him back?

Charlotte asked him the same question. 'Don't you want to?'

'Of course I want to. Very much.'

'Then?'

Then…nothing? Before the doubt in his mind could speak one more word, Ben slid his arms around Charlotte's waist and pulled her tight. Their lips met before he could take a breath. Soft, wet, eager.

They continued the conversation with the kiss, their tongues saying everything that needed to be said.

I want this.

I want you.

Charlotte's bikini hid nothing. When he slid his hands down her back, he felt only glorious, soft skin. When her hands explored him, she felt only his bare chest, with his heart hammering like a drum under his ribs. And it was wonderful. Everything he'd never let himself dream.

But as her fingers began to explore the waistband of his shorts he realised they were approaching the point of no return. A friendship might survive a few kisses, but the next step would be different. He lifted his mouth from hers.

'Charlotte, you know that if you keep doing that, everything will change,' he murmured with his last breath of restraint.

'I thought you wanted it too.' She slid her palm down his back and into the waistband of his shorts.

'I do. Very much. I'm just checking in with you again.'

'Ben, if today is anything to go by, I'd say something in our friendship has already changed.' She moved her hand from the back of his shorts and to the front, her fingertips coming so close to him he could feel their warmth.

She was right; the kisses had already made things strained between them. But what they were going to do next would change it again. He knew that he couldn't make love to her and walk away. Once they crossed this line, any lies that he might have told himself about his feelings for her would be shown to be that: a convenient fabrication to protect his own heart.

'Promise me we'll keep talking?'

'Why wouldn't we?'

'I mean, keep talking with one another about how we're feeling. That way if things start to get weird, or strange or uncomfortable, we can deal with it.'

'Of course.'

'Promise me,' he insisted. 'As long as we let one another know how we're feeling, we'll be okay.'

'I promise.' Charlotte nodded.

He exhaled and Charlotte lifted a hand behind her back, untying the knot of her bikini with a single tug. She shed her bikini to clear the last remaining distance between them, shattering the last of Ben's remaining resolve.

This was it. It was happening.

He lifted his hand to her bare shoulder and rubbed her tender skin with the pad of his thumb, mirroring her motion from moments earlier. Her eyelids lowered, and she exhaled. Exquisite. She was perfect. He lowered his mouth to her shoulder and kissed it. She tasted of sunshine and desire. His lips traced their way slowly across her collarbone and he felt her shoulders shiver. He was going to explore every inch, every curve, every corner of her.

Ben tilted his head and met Charlotte's gaze. Her eyes lowered to his lips and hers beckoned. Slowly, savouring each moment of anticipation, their mouths gradually came together again.

Tasting, exploring. Their tongues slid together in a beautiful dance. Charlotte leaned further into him and he felt her sighs vibrate through her.

He was aware of her hands moving slowly tentatively over his body, down his back, pushing down his shorts. Realising his knees might give way at any moment, he scooped her up and carried her to her room.

He laid her on her bed and she pulled him on top of her, her warmth exhilarating beneath him. She wrapped her legs around him, pulling him even tighter to her. Only his shorts and her skimpy bikini bottoms lay between them, but their thin fabric was a technicality only; his hand slipped under the wet fabric and over her gorgeous buttocks. They could both tell how aroused he was through his wet shorts. They had never been closer, or more intimate. He lowered his head and took one of Charlotte's perfect and perfectly erect nipples between his lips and even at that simple touch her back arched and she moaned. Her restraint was even thinner than his.

He lifted his mouth away.

'No, Ben, don't stop. Please.'

When she begged, he gave in. Who was he to deny her something that they both craved? Something that felt so perfect. He lowered his mouth again, pleasuring one breast and then the other, while Charlotte's fingers carefully relieved him of his shorts and stroked his length so perfectly he worried he would embarrass himself.

When he thought her touch might shatter him, he wriggled away...and trailed kisses down her belly, to the hem of her bikini bottoms. He eased them lower, breathing hard, shaking as he did so.

Charlotte... Charlotte... he repeated over and over in his head.

This was Charlotte. He'd never even let himself contemplate the next step.

He must have been too slow for Charlotte because she wriggled herself out of them, revealing the last of her beautiful body to him, confident, eager and without the slightest hesitation. He lowered his head, tasted her, heard her soft moans, and stroked her over and over again.

She nudged his head away and said, 'Stay right where you are.'

'Where are you going?'

'Two feet to the left to get a condom from my bag. Don't even think of moving.'

Her direction was firm. She was ordering him not to change his mind at the final hurdle. His head started to spin and he rolled onto his back. She was right to warn him. This was the point where either of them could stop and change their mind.

He sighed. No, he couldn't. He was too deep in. He'd felt Charlotte, tasted her.

The next step was already inevitable.

He insisted on sheathing himself, not trusting himself to hold himself together if Charlotte's fingers slid over him again at this point. He found her mouth again and kissed her, harder this time, as her legs wrapped around him, pulled him against her. Instinctively, they knew what the other wanted.

She was ready. He'd been ready for years and could only hope he didn't disappoint her.

He was hoping to hold himself together for as long as she was going to need, but didn't anticipate she would reach her climax so quickly, so forcefully. He fell mere seconds after her, as her body was still shaking. Pleasure tore through him like a blaze but he held her, kept her safe, kept her steady.

When his peak subsided, it took him a moment to realise over the waves of his own climax that Charlotte was still shaking, but his shoulder suddenly felt wet, and he realised she was crying.

CHAPTER SIX

CHARLOTTE'S BODY FLOODED with pleasure, it coursed through her, more powerful, deeper than she'd known in years. But one convulsion was slowly replaced with another, more unstoppable, unexpected vibration.

Rising in her throat, pushing behind her eyes, filling the back of her nose.

The vibrations were no longer orgasm, but sobs. They rose up through her and shook her even as she was still lying tangled in Ben's arms.

He rubbed her back in soothing circles, realising what was happening even before she did.

She swallowed and gasped and tried to hold the tears in but they came from somewhere deep, hidden behind a wall she hadn't even known was there, and flooded her uncontrollably.

'It's okay, it's okay,' Ben whispered.

But it wasn't okay at all.

It was shocking. Mortifying.

She pulled herself up and turned away from him. It was a wrench, but it was necessary. She took deep breaths to steady her body and turn back the tears. She grabbed the sheet and wiped her face, vaguely aware of Ben lying on the bed behind her as she pulled herself together.

'Oh, God, Ben, I'm so sorry. I'm so embarrassed.'

'Don't be,' he said gruffly.

'No, I am, I don't know where that came from. I don't know what just happened.'

'It's all right, really.' Ben sat up behind her pressed a quick kiss on her bare shoulder before grabbing his shorts and leaving the room.

She caught a glimpse of his bare arse as he left and the feeling stirred inside her again. She was attracted to Ben, deeply, crazily attracted.

But it was attraction laced with more bitter emotions.

Embarrassment.

Shock.

Guilt.

She groaned and flopped back onto her bed.

She stared at the ceiling, the intricate patterns carved in the wood, and tried to figure out what on earth had just happened.

She had nothing to feel guilty about. Embarrassed, yes. But not guilty.

She was willing, Ben was willing.

Sex had not been like that for her in years. Not since Tim.

The tears rose back up again but Charlotte quickly got off her bed and went to the bathroom.

She splashed her face with cold water and washed them away.

Maybe these tears, this pounding in her chest was about Tim after all? She'd run away from the London autumn but couldn't really escape the feelings that swamped her each year.

What if this new attraction to Ben was simply a symptom of her grief? A way of trying to forget about Tim.

If so, it had backfired spectacularly.

But sex with Ben was good.

No, sex with Ben was *great*.

Sex with Ben had opened up a place she'd forgotten was even there. The place where you were at one with each other, entirely attuned to the other person. Where the other person knew you so well, they knew exactly how to hold you, touch you, stimulate you.

Opening up that place had surprised her. She hadn't even realised what had come over her until it was too late.

She was such a fool. And poor Ben! She'd practically begged him to sleep with her, promised it wouldn't change their friendship and then this had happened.

Charlotte ran herself a bath and sat on the edge while she waited for it to fill.

Outside her room she heard a door bang. The front door. It was dark outside, but Ben must have gone out. She buried her face in her hands and groaned. She'd messed things up spectacularly. Pursued her best friend and then cried after the best sex she'd had in years.

As long as we let one another know how we're feeling, we'll be okay.

It was just as well he'd left, because she didn't know the first thing to say to him. She didn't even understand what was going on herself.

She slipped into the warm relaxing bath.

When Ben got back the first thing she needed to do was explain that the crying was not a review of his love-making ability. Quite the opposite. Ben's hands had known just the right pressure to apply, his fingers had known just where to stroke her. He'd been attentive, focused. Caring.

He'd known just where to touch her. And that had been the problem. No other man had been able to reach her there. Not since Tim.

The warm bath, the long day, the love-making, all conspired to make her drowsy. She pulled herself out of the bath, put on her pyjamas and opened her bedroom door so she would hear Ben's return. Once he was back, they would talk. She fell onto her bed, spent and exhausted, and she slept.

It was morning when Charlotte woke and saw the door to her room was closed. Ben must have closed it when he returned. She opened it slowly and padded out into the main room. Ben's side of the villa was quiet and his door was closed as well.

She wanted to walk across the foyer, open his door and slip into his bed, just to hold him and feel his warmth against her body.

But he didn't want that. He probably wanted space, which was why he'd left last night.

No wonder. What must he think? She hadn't just cried, she'd sobbed uncontrollably. She would explain, but he had to be ready to hear it, and clearly he wasn't. She had no idea how late he'd got back last night. She had no recollection of him returning to the villa. Where had he gone? For a walk? To a bar?

You pushed him away. You shouldn't be surprised if he took himself off for a drink or four.

She turned back to her room, slipped on a dress. She needed coffee. And food. She'd skipped dinner and with all of yesterday evening's excitement neither of them had placed a breakfast order. She'd go get coffee, bring one back for Ben and then they would talk.

Charlotte hadn't slept with too many people, but enough to know that last night she had made a terrible faux pas. It wasn't even as though the sex had been tear-worthy, just the opposite, but she didn't know how to explain that to Ben without sounding silly.

Making love to you was so good I had to sob my eyes out.

She needed to come up with something that made more sense than that.

Charlotte was surprised to see Summer at the nearest cafe, sitting on the deck, writing in a notepad.

'Hey there,' she said.

Summer looked up and her face lit up. 'Hi.'

'I'm just going to grab breakfast. Would you like to join me?' Charlotte looked around. 'Unless you're meeting Will?'

'No, I mean, yes, please stay. I just ordered a coffee.'

Charlotte pulled out a chair. 'Where's Will?'

'I'm honestly not sure.'

Charlotte nodded, but didn't say more, remembering Ben's concern that something was not quite right between Will and Summer.

The two women drank their coffee then ordered some breakfast. Charlotte ordered a sweet Indonesian porridge with coconut milk, ginger and sugar. It was delicious but she also salivated over Summer's order of *bubur ayam*, which was a type of rice, with chicken and sliced boiled egg on top.

With food and coffee in her, Charlotte's mood brightened, but she still felt unsteady. Her new attraction to Ben was confusing and threatening to destabilise their friendship. She could rule out alcohol. Her jet lag had passed. That left hormone fluctuations. But those had never made her react like this in the past.

'Is thirty too young for perimenopause?' Charlotte blurted out.

Summer snorted. 'I'm not an expert, but maybe. Why?'

'Because I feel strange. Like my hormones are off balance.'

'You're not pregnant, are you? That's more likely in someone your age than perimenopause.'

Pregnant? Charlotte almost choked on her coffee. Even if she was pregnant, it would be way too early to know. Besides, they had used protection. And she had an IUD.

But what if she were pregnant? With Ben's baby? Ben would make a wonderful father. She touched her stomach. The thought of having Ben's baby didn't make her distressed. Strangely, it made her calm. Would it have Ben's gorgeous curls? His bright blue eyes? His dimple?

Where was she?

Charlotte shook her head and returned to the conversation. 'No,' she answered.

Summer laughed. 'That looked like you aren't quite sure if you could be pregnant or not.'

'No, I'm not pregnant, it's not that.'

Summer grinned. 'Are you and Ben…? I thought you were just friends.'

Discussions about new relationships were usually the sort of conversations she had with Ben, but of course she couldn't have this conversation with Ben. Not when it was her feelings for him she was trying to figure out. But Summer already felt like a friend, and Charlotte desperately needed to speak with someone about what had happened.

'It's new.'

Summer's eyes widened.

'It's very, very new,' Charlotte added.

'That's exciting.' Summer leaned closer. 'Congratulations.'

'But it's confusing and…scary.'

'Scary? Why?'

'Because it's Ben. He's my best friend.'

'That's the best way to start something.'

'Is it? Because it feels terrifying.'

'Why?'

Charlotte took a deep breath. She might as well tell Summer everything. 'I had a boyfriend once, we were engaged. But he died.'

'Oh, no, I'm so sorry.'

Charlotte nodded. It was her standard response. She never really knew what to say, especially when someone who didn't even know Tim expressed sympathy. 'I don't want to hurt like that again. I want to find someone, have a partner. But I just don't think I can go through losing someone again. And because it's Ben, it's as though the stakes are higher than ever.'

Her best friend, the man whose company she felt most comfortable in, was also a wonderful lover. She should feel over-the-moon excited, but the overwhelming feeling she had right now was fear. Fear that she would lose Ben one way or another. Fear she would mess up this new part of their relationship.

Fear Ben might decide it had all been a mistake.

Or…

There were plenty of things that might happen to cause her to lose Ben for good. She didn't want to make a complete list.

'Is Ben pressuring you? Does he want more than you can give right now?'

'No, see, that's just it. I don't think he does. He's the one holding back. I'm the one with the crazy hormonal stuff going on.'

Summer laughed. 'My advice, for what it's worth, would be not to think too hard about these things. Feel more, think less. I think you're in safe hands with Ben.'

Safe hands. Lean, strong hands. Talented hands. The memory of them on her breasts the night before flashed into her mind and her muscles clenched.

'You don't have to know where you're going to end up, you don't have to know the future from the start. Because no one ever does.'

Charlotte nodded. Summer was right; even the best-laid plans could unravel in front of you, under the wheels of a lorry. She just had to see how things went with Ben. She had to give it a try.

She would go back to the villa, Ben would be

awake and they would talk and make things right. They had to. Their friendship was too important. Charlotte downed the last of her coffee. She was going to go back and talk to Ben. Try to explain what had happened the night before. Tell him how she felt. What was the worst that could happen?

She stood and heard a voice. Diane.

'Just the two ladies I wanted to see,' she said. 'I hope you're both ready to party.'

I don't know what just happened.

Charlotte might have been surprised by her tears. She might not have understood.

But Ben did. He knew exactly what was wrong.

She wasn't ready.

By the time Charlotte had peeled her warm, shaking body away from his, he, too, was close to tears.

Making love with Charlotte had nearly ripped him apart as well, but for a different reason. Ever since he'd first met Charlotte he'd known, on some level, that he needed to keep her at a distance—emotionally and physically. He'd known that Charlotte had the capacity to break his heart irreparably. He'd understood that she was not ready to open her heart again, and maybe she never would be.

And now it was more important to remember that than ever: sex with Charlotte might have been good, it might have even been great, but that was all it was. A sexual need. A physical desire. Nothing more.

He left her room, tided himself up, slipped on shorts and a T-shirt. Then he stood outside her room and paced. Past the rumpled bed, probably still warm from their bodies, he could see the bathroom door was closed.

He heard the bath start to run, a massive tub, identical to the one in his room. It would take ages to fill.

Charlotte might be content in the bath, but the four walls of his room were closing in on him. He slipped on his shoes, grabbed the room key and left.

The road near the villa was different at night, and so different from London. It was much quieter, and very dark. He was a world and a tumultuous week away from where he was when he first learned of his mother's wedding.

If Charlotte hadn't decided to come with him, she'd be back in London and none of this would have happened, and things would be as they were between them. Safe. Steady. Stable.

Is that what you want? To go back in time a week? For this never to have happened?

Maybe.

As amazing as the last few hours had been, they had still been a mistake. As perfectly wonderful as it had been to hold one another, entirely bare themselves to each other, Charlotte hadn't been ready.

She wasn't over Tim.

Of course she's not over Tim, he scolded himself. *If she was, she wouldn't have wanted to escape the rainy British autumn to come to the other side of the world with you!*

As a rule, Ben avoided self-reflection when it came to his feelings for Charlotte, afraid of what he might find if he analysed his heart too closely. He tried not to now, but thought and worries kept resurfacing—despite his best efforts to push them away, they bobbed up like a buoy.

You love her. You're in love with Charlotte.

He shook his head.

He couldn't love her; they didn't have that kind of relationship.

He wouldn't love her, it would ruin everything.

His mind was just confused after making love with her. Scratch that, his mind was confused after having sex with her.

Energy coursed through him and he walked on and on. The night air was cooler before he knew it. He'd covered so much distance he'd reached a part of the island they hadn't been to before. Below him he could hear waves crashing into cliffs.

He had no idea how long he'd been walking, having left his phone and watch back at the villa. All he had on him was the villa key card.

Charlotte probably needed her space anyway. She needed time to process what had happened as much as he had. Maybe more.

But what if Charlotte's way of processing involved up and leaving? It wasn't an inconceivable idea; Charlotte did have form for running away whenever a man got too close.

If she does leave while you're out, you know where to find her in London.

Far from reassuring him, the thought made him worry even further. Just because he knew where she lived and worked didn't mean she'd want to speak to him.

Ben resisted the urge to scream at the sea.

He knew she wasn't ready! Why did he let himself get pulled into that situation? Of course he wanted to kiss her, hold her, be with her—he always had—but he'd never let himself because he knew, deep down, this was exactly where he'd end up.

Not on this dark beach in Bali, exactly, but alone, with Charlotte panicking somewhere else. Ready to flee. Suddenly overcome with exhaustion, he let his knees buckle and he sat on a nearby bench.

Ben was always going to be second best. He saw that now.

Second best to Will.

Second best to Tim.

He'd never be the man Charlotte wanted and

that was all there was. He had to accept that and get on with his life. He couldn't change his father's feelings and he'd never change Charlotte's.

All he could do was get on with things the best he could.

He moved his breath in time with the waves—in and out, in and out. He wasn't happy, not by any stretch, but he was calmer.

Ben made his way slowly back to the villa, rehearsing what he was going to say to her.

Charlotte, I'm sorry. Can we pretend this never happened?

That was laughable—pretending wasn't helpful when they needed to be honest.

Charlotte, I'm sorry, I know you still love Tim. I can move past this if you can.

But could he? Could he continue to be her friend, sit across from her at her gallery or in some London cafe and not think of the red bikini?

Charlotte, I'm sorry. If it isn't too strange for you, I'd really like us to remain friends. Please tell me what I can do to save our friendship.

That was it, that was what he had to say. She might never be his lover, but he couldn't lose her from his life for ever.

He unlocked the door and took a deep breath, his heart pounding so hard his ribs ached. But Charlotte wasn't in the living room. His heart picked up speed. *Please don't let her have left.*

The door to her room was wide open and Charlotte was fast asleep, sprawled out in short shorts and a tank top on top of the unmade bed. He could hear her deep, steady breathing from the doorway.

He watched her, wondering if she would wake, but she didn't. He covered her with a sheet and closed her door quietly behind him and went to his own.

Ben lay on his cold bed and at some stage his mind succumbed to the needs of his body, and he fell into a deep dreamless sleep.

He woke, disoriented, not knowing what time it was or even what hemisphere he was in.

Ben stretched, splashed water in his face and went to speak to her.

Please tell me what I can do to save our friendship.

A figure sat at the table by the pool, looking at the view. But it wasn't Charlotte.

It was his mother.

CHAPTER SEVEN

'LIKE A HEN NIGHT?' Ben asked.

'It's not really a hen night, it's more a women's afternoon, and Gus is having a gathering with just the men. He'd really like you to join them.'

It seemed unnecessarily traditional to Ben, but what really worried him was that it meant more time without seeing Charlotte. Where was she now? He looked past his mother to Charlotte's room. The door was open, but it was empty. He'd know if Charlotte was in the villa, he'd be able to sense her.

He was such a fool, sleeping so late. Letting her go.

'Do you know where Charlotte is?' He tried to keep his voice neutral.

'Don't you?' Diane asked.

'No, I just woke up.'

His mother gave him an unreadable look.

'She had breakfast with Summer, and now they're doing some things for me. Helping me with the party.'

The relief he felt was physical; Charlotte hadn't left the island. She was simply with Summer.

'Please go. I'd really like you and Will to have a chance to get to know Gus without me. And besides, I'd like to spend some time with Summer and Charlotte. They tell me more about my sons than my sons do themselves.'

Ben was going to open his mouth to remind his mother that he and Charlotte were not dating like Summer and Will, but he held his tongue again.

What would he tell his mother anyway? How could he explain what was going on between them when he wasn't even sure himself? They weren't dating, but were they still friends? Could their friendship recover from earth-shaking sex that had ended in tears?

In the bright light of day his fears from last night had not disappeared. They seemed as rational as ever. Running away was what Charlotte did. She'd dumped other men for far less than tears after sex. Not liking the way he chewed. Living on the other side of the city…

'So you'll go? To Gus's shindig?'

Do I have a choice? he wanted to mumble, like a teenager. But he knew the answer. Charlotte would be busy with Summer and his mother. Even if she wanted to talk, which seemed unlikely, she couldn't.

At least this way, Charlotte was less likely to abscond.

Ben nodded. He and Charlotte would have to talk later.

'Will's going too,' Diane added.

That wasn't a positive.

'It'll be good for you to spend some time together.'

Ben wanted to contradict his mother but bit it back; he and Will were practically strangers, ever since Will had supported their father's decision to cut Ben off and Ben had left Australia.

He expected his mother to leave, now that he'd promised to spend the afternoon with Gus, but Diane stayed seated.

'Ben, darling, I'm so glad that you came for the wedding. I know it isn't easy for you. And I know that Gus and I are doing this quickly.'

'Yes,' Ben said. 'Why is that exactly?'

'Because we love one another.'

Yes, but that didn't mean you got married instantly. 'Sure, but why the rush?'

'Because you never know what's around the corner.'

Ben didn't feel like arguing with that. Something around a corner could jump out and upend your life in a few hours of reckless passion. His next question came out in a rush. 'Were you and Dad happy?'

Diane pulled a face. 'Why do you ask?'

'Because I'm curious, but you can tell me to mind my own business if you like.'

Diane considered his question.

'We were. But…'

She looked at the ocean, as though the answer were there. His mother's hesitation made him sad. And more than a little angry at his dead father.

Diane sighed. 'I wasn't unhappy, but things were not always easy between us. He was obsessed with his company and put it first. You know that.'

All too well. 'And?'

'I didn't always agree with all of your father's decisions.'

But you went along with them, Ben thought bitterly.

'Like deciding not to pay my tuition?'

'That was difficult. You know your father thought that since you didn't plan on working in the business, there was no reason for him to pay for your studies. It was a business decision, not a personal one.'

But it *was* still personal. Saying it was a 'business decision' was just his father's way of trying to manipulate Ben into giving up his dreams and passion and falling into line.

'I know that it looked as though your father was favouring Will.'

'It didn't just look like it, he was.'

Diane sighed. 'I think he really wanted to protect you.'

'How?'

'You chose a tough road, Ben. And I know you have done amazingly, but a decade ago, fresh out of school, I think your father though that the best chance you had to lead a stable and happy life was to choose the safe option.'

'Working for him.'

'Yes. I know he could have handled things better. *We* could have handled things better. But I think he truly just wanted you to come and work with him and Will.'

Ben thought it over.

No. It was his mother rewriting history. Trying to forget all the other things his father had done over the years. Withholding not just support, but also love.

'It wasn't just about the money. It was everything.' His father would ask Will about his studies, his life. Each time he'd see Ben he'd refer to him as a freeloader or lazy. Or ungrateful. 'He belittled me. Made fun of my dreams. But Will? There was nothing he wouldn't do for Will.'

Diane pursed her lips together.

'But it wasn't Will's doing. It wasn't his fault.'

No, it wasn't Will's fault. And it wasn't even their mother's; Diane had always showered Ben with affection and treated him exactly as she'd treated Will.

Ben still seethed. He'd had a privileged upbringing, but his father's love had been conditional. Maybe he was being petulant, still holding a grudge about something like his university tuition. Or the car. And the apartment he'd bought for Will. Maybe. But it still hurt. Being second best hurt. And now his father was gone the emotions were just as complex, still uncomfortable. No wonder he stayed away from his family. It was easier than dealing with them.

'But then why rush into marrying Gus?' Realising his question might have overstepped a line, Ben rushed on. 'I'm not disapproving, but I want to make sure you're okay.'

Diane picked up his hand and squeezed it.

'Your father and I were happy. I loved him very much. But it is possible to love more than one person in your life.'

Was it? Ben wanted to ask. That hadn't been his experience at all.

Ben showered and dressed for the afternoon with Gus and his friends.

A knock at the door sent his heart into his windpipe. Charlotte was back! He yanked open the door, but it wasn't Charlotte. It was his brother. Looking annoyed.

'Are you ready?'

'For Gus's thing?'

'Yeah, Mum said you were coming too.'

'I was waiting for Charlotte.'

'She's already at Mum's.'

Ben's throat closed over. Even Will knew where

Charlotte was, when Ben didn't. She was avoiding him. It was clear.

Ben contemplated giving Will an excuse and
begging off Gus's thing, but Will was giving him
a look that was saying, 'Get yourself together.'

Despite being the same height, Will still somehow managed to stare at Ben as though he were
looking down at him.

'Let's go. The sooner we get there, the sooner
we can leave.'

His logic was sound. And then, Will added
softly, 'She's with Summer. They're together,
they'll be fine.'

Something inside Ben uncoiled. His brother
was right.

Across the bay, the lights from another bar sparkled. Charlotte was there.

Now that the sun had set, the afternoon was
definitely over. Will was talking to Gus's father,
no doubt about something business-related that
would put Ben to sleep. Ben figured he'd served
his time. He'd waited long enough to see Charlotte and with each moment that passed he felt
more and more on edge.

'You're not leaving already?' Gus said when
Ben bade him goodnight.

Ben nodded. 'Congratulations.'

Gus, several beers in, unexpectedly pulled him
into a hug. 'I'm really looking forward to getting

to know you better. I know this is awkward, but
I love your mother more than anything in the
world. There's nothing I wouldn't do for her.'

'I know that,' Ben said. It wasn't a lie. Gus did
seem like a great guy and his mother deserved
to be happy.

'So stay?'

Ben shook his head. 'I have to talk to Charlotte.'

'Is everything okay? Sorry, you don't have to
tell me. But you can. Unless that's weird?'

Gus's earnestness was endearing. He was nothing like Ben's father—they were polar opposites.
*That's probably what my mother loves about
him.*

His mother hadn't found a replacement for his
autocratic father, but a gentler, calmer man and
Ben was relieved. For everyone's sake.

The only thing that made him sad was the
past: his mother being married to a man who saw
family decisions as business transactions. If you
weren't in the business, you weren't in the family.

'I'm not sure if Diane told you, but we're planning on coming to London in a few months,' Gus
said.

Ben shook his head. 'She didn't mention it.'

'Well, we are. She'd love to see you again; we
both would. And Charlotte too. But I'd better let
you get back to her now,' Gus said with a wink
and Ben didn't mind the implication at all. He

was going to find Charlotte and finally talk about what had happened last night.

Ben's heart hammered against his ribs. He felt his pulse in a hundred places throughout his body as he waited outside the restaurant for Charlotte. He'd sent her a message asking if she wanted to walk home with him, but she hadn't answered and he had no idea if she was still at the party. Even less idea whether she would want to speak to him, but a few beers with Gus and the boys had given him the extra nudge of courage he needed. They had to talk at some point, didn't they?

Then there she was. Wearing a short floral dress, her hair tied up loosely on her head, her face flushed.

She smiled at him and it felt as though he was breathing properly for the first time that day.

'Hey,' he said.

'Hey.'

'I thought you might like someone to walk home with.' The sunlight still lingered in the west, but it would be dark by the time they reached the villa.

'You're not kicking on with the boys?'

'No, it was remarkably restrained.'

Charlotte laughed. 'Unlike Diane's do.'

'Do you want to stay?'

'No! I was ready to leave. I'm exhausted.'

They walked along the dark path, occasional lights and half a moon guiding their way.

'I'm sorry,' they said simultaneously.

They laughed and before she could say anything he began the speech he'd been rehearsing all day.

'I'm so sorry, Charlotte. I know you're still upset about Tim.'

She kept walking and kicked the ground a few times with her feet. When she finally spoke she said, 'Ah, no, I don't think that's it. You see, I think my reaction last night was the opposite.'

'What do you mean?'

'I mean, I didn't cry because I was sad about Tim. I was crying because I wasn't. Sad about him. I was crying because I finally wasn't holding back.'

Ben had failed exams that made more sense than what Charlotte was saying.

'I still don't understand. Holding what back?'

'You know…' Charlotte made a rolling motion with her right hand.

'No, I don't.'

She stopped walking. 'Ben, I've been on a lot of dates but it's never…never been like that. They never made me feel like you did. I never managed to…' Charlotte made the rolling motion with her hands again.

'Orgasm?' he asked, so there could be no doubt what she was saying.

'Yes.' Charlotte looked down, as though she was embarrassed.

She'd cried because she'd climaxed. And no other man she'd been with since Tim had done that? Except him. At that moment Ben felt a hundred feet tall and would have taken on any predator that approached them. Seven-foot body-builder? He'd take him on. Angry tiger? Let him at 'em.

'Oh, I see.' Ben tried to keep his voice even. 'You're not upset about it?'

'No, well, I'm embarrassed.'

'You don't need to be, really.'

'Ben, come on. Me bursting into tears must have seemed like a pretty brutal review of what we'd done, but that wasn't it at all.'

Feeling happier than he had since the previous evening, Ben almost didn't hear what Charlotte said next. 'So, I was wondering if...'

Ben stopped walking.

'I was wondering if you would give me an-other chance.'

'Another chance?'

'Yes, Ben, I'm sorry and... I thought maybe I won't mess it up next time.'

Was she suggesting what he hadn't even dared to hope?

'You want to...again?'

'I think I do. That is...only if you do?'

'Yes, I do.' And because those words were not

enough to convey how he was really feeling, he added, 'Very much.'

Ben's hand was shaking when he lifted the key card to the lock. Charlotte lifted her hand to steady his and held his hand as he pressed the card to the lock and the door clicked open.

He reached for her, slid his hands around her waist, then down over her hips and up her body again. Charlotte wrapped her arms around his neck and he felt her fingertips slip into his hair.

He kissed the soft skin of her neck. The place he'd studied hundreds of times. He tasted it, breathed in her scent, inhaled until she completely filled his lungs.

All day she'd thought he was avoiding her. Waiting until she was asleep to return to the villa, waiting for her to leave before getting up. Or maybe she'd been avoiding him. She certainly hadn't been looking forward to the conversation they had to have, fearing he'd be upset. Or worse, that he would say they mustn't begin a physical relationship.

But there he was, waiting outside the bar for her. Hands in his pockets, looking nervous. Shy. And her heart exploded. Every worry, every concern, every fear she'd had evaporated at that moment. He wasn't upset; confused maybe, but he wanted to listen to what she had to say.

Last night had been a major turning point for

her. Not just because Ben had brought her to climax, though that had been unexpected, but because she'd realised that the reason he'd been able to do that was because this was right between them.

He might be trying to be sensible by giving her space, by taking things slowly, but that couldn't change the fact that whatever was going on between them was right. She was excited about this new thing between them and maybe she was being a little reckless, but her body throbbed with desire for him. His lips were on her neck and her insides were already molten as he kicked the door to the villa closed.

His kisses stayed restrained at first, but as she pushed deeper, he followed. His hands stayed in a chaste zone, but hers slid down his hips and to his bottom.

He mirrored her actions. Quickly followed her lead.

She slid her hands under his shirt to feel his hard, muscular back. She tried to ease his shirt up but Ben shifted position so she couldn't. Never mind, she'd head in the other direction. Her fingertips slid under the waistband of his shorts and began to manipulate the button.

His kisses stopped and her neck went cold.

He's holding back. He doesn't want this.

'Are you okay?' Her voice trembled. She wanted this. She wanted him.

'Yes.' He nodded. 'Are you?'

'Never better,' she murmured.

He paused and looked deep into her eyes.

Then he scooped her up and carried her to his bed. He pulled his shirt off in a movement so swift she was surprised not to hear ripping fabric. Then she gazed at his broad chest. Abs. Ben had abs. She lifted her finger and traced them.

'Did you always have these?'

'As far as I know.'

'You might have told me.'

'You never asked,' he murmured against her chest, his kisses exploring lower and lower.

He pulled her dress over her head and the air hit her skin for a moment only before he covered her with his warm body. They kissed and kissed, her body growing tighter, wetter, more impatient. Ben moved lower, ran his hands over her breasts then took them one at a time into his mouth. She stifled a moan.

She wanted him.

Needed him. Like air. As soon as possible.

Ben unbuttoned his shorts and slid them over his hips, but before he could kick them off, she reached greedily for him, rubbing her hand over him, feeling the length of his arousal, every muscle between her legs tightening. He was tender, yet firm. His kisses delicate, his body hard. Every muscle in her body reacted to him, from the ones in her toes to the ones in her heart.

He scrambled for his bag and a condom, even as she straddled him.

Ben's eyes widened in appreciation as she moved on top of him. She knew what was coming, knew, with a certainty that she hadn't felt in years that Ben could satisfy her, bring her to an earth-shaking climax. But even as he moved inside her, touched parts of her that no one had been able to reach, she knew she never wanted this to end. The orgasm would be the icing on the cake, being close to Ben, feeling him, tasting him, was the main event.

'Don't hold back,' she said. She wasn't talking about his body, but he didn't need to know that.

Don't hold back, let every part of yourself go. I want all of you.

She reached a climax before him, but rather than the reaction the evening before, she was revitalised, and pulled him even closer to her, rocking, marvelling at what it was like to make love with her best friend. Marvelling at the way he felt against her and the look on his face when he too broke apart.

Ben slept next to her, flat out on his stomach. She watched his beautiful back rise and fall with each gentle, contented breath.

Her heart tugged towards him. What on earth was going on with them? It was wonderful and terrifying all at once. Last night's love-making had not been a one-off. Ben had shown her, again and again this evening, that he could make her body feel things she hadn't felt in years.

And he was having the same effect on her heart as well.

Was it possible to fall in love so quickly?

Of course, it hadn't all been fast, they'd known one another for years, but three days was very fast to go from platonic friendship to love.

Love.

She pushed the word aside. It wasn't a helpful word to use. Of course she loved Ben. But love as a friend, or as a person, was very different from making love, falling in love.

This was lust and need and desire.

This was wanting to spend every moment with him, waking and sleeping. This was also touching her belly and thinking back to what Summer had asked her.

Are you pregnant?

She wasn't, they'd been careful again, but the idea of carrying Ben's baby didn't fill her with fear or dread, and now that the idea had been planted in her mind, she couldn't shake it.

Did *that* mean she was falling in love with him?

How was it possible to know someone for years and then suddenly fall in love? The idea felt strange and reckless. Unlikely, even impossible.

Risking waking him, she slid her hand over his warm back and rested it on his muscular shoulder.

Ben wasn't reckless. That was why he was being the sensible one and holding back, because he knew that three days was far too fast for their feelings to change like this.

Ben was cautious, he hadn't been swept up in whatever tropical fever had taken over her. Ben was her best friend and now she knew he was a great lover. She wanted to stay up all night watching him sleep, but she had to check herself, pull her feelings in.

Because what if Ben didn't fall at the same speed she found herself plummeting? Where would she be then? Awkwardly in love with her best friend while he just carried on unaffected.

Ben kept his feelings so close to his chest, she would have to tread carefully, but she needed to know how he felt and whether she had to protect her heart, or whether she could let herself fall, knowing that he would be there to catch her. She lay down and pressed her cheek to his shoulder. Safe, firm. She couldn't lose him.

Tomorrow she would make him open up.

CHAPTER EIGHT

THE FIRST RAYS of sunlight began streaming into Ben's room. Charlotte marvelled at how it hit his soft brown hair and brought out every highlight. She lay on her stomach next to him with her chin resting on his shoulder blade and drew circles across his back.

This man was gorgeous. Everything about this moment was gorgeous. The new day, the new relationship and sense of completeness in her chest. This was where she was meant to be.

Ben rolled over onto his back with a groan.

'Are you okay?' she asked.

'Never better,' he replied groggily.

'You don't sound like it.'

He met her gaze and smiled. 'We just didn't get much sleep last night.'

'It's almost like we're not even on Indonesian time,' Charlotte agreed. She kissed a sweet spot just behind his ear. 'I think we should just stay in bed all day.'

She loved this, the freedom to touch and feel

any part of him she wanted. And it was all the more amazing because this wasn't some random stranger that she didn't know and didn't trust, this was Ben, who she could trust with her own life. And maybe even her heart.

But she still had to be careful. The new day hadn't brought any more certainty to her about the new nature of their relationship.

Yes, they were friends. Yes, they were physically compatible, but did he have the same feeling of a swarm of butterflies in his stomach as she had? Did he feel the same racing in his heart each time he looked at her?

'We do have a wedding to go to the day after tomorrow though.' Ben pulled himself away slightly from her kisses and her heart dropped.

'You're not freaking out about this?' she asked carefully.

Ben laughed. 'Me? Freaking out? You're the one most likely to panic.'

Charlotte sat up and pulled the sheet to her chest. 'What do you mean? Why would I panic?'

Ben shook his head. 'Never mind. I'm sorry, that came out wrong.'

But she understood. He was being careful and making sure that she wasn't falling too fast. It was his way of saying, 'We need to take this one day at a time.'

He was right. Even though she was ready to give

him all of her heart, she knew it was happening very quickly.

Charlotte traced a line from his eyes down his cheek to his chin and then around his lips. 'I'm not freaking out,' she whispered and planted a quick kiss on his lips before going to the bathroom.

When she emerged, Ben was dressed in shorts, but nothing else and sitting on the deck overlooking the pool and the ocean. If she had her way, this was how he would dress, always.

He passed her a fresh cup of coffee. 'What do you want to do today?'

'I want to stay here.'

And just look at you. I don't want to share you with anyone.

Ben grinned.

'We have to go to that thing tonight.' Gus and Diane were really making the most of having all of their friends and family in the one place and had organised yet another gathering. This time all the wedding guests were invited.

'I know, but until then, we could stay here.'

'Are you sure?' he asked.

She felt a stab of guilt at the fact he might want to make the most of their short visit to Bali, so she said, 'But we can play tourist if you like.'

He gave her a knowing grin and shook his head. 'There's nowhere else in the world I'd rather be.'

* * *

They drank their coffee and ate some breakfast, but only for long enough to gather their energy before they returned to the bedroom. This time it was Charlotte who fell asleep afterwards, feeling safe and secure in Ben's arms.

But she was alone in her bed when she awoke many hours later and the sense of security she'd felt earlier had vanished, replaced again with the uncertainty that was slowly but surely gnawing at her. She told herself to take a breath, let things take their course, but it was hard to reach that stage of Zen. Even with the scene she found when she walked out onto the deck. Ben, with his feet up, head facing the sky, eyes closed. The sun dancing across the water of the pool and the azure ocean. If she didn't feel calm here, what chance did she have in the bustle of London, when they went back to their normal lives?

Charlotte sat on the day bed and stretched out, letting the sun warm her limbs as well. After a while, Ben stirred and noticed her beside him. The smile that broke across his face made her stomach swoop.

'How are you doing?'

His question was open and honest, and she was almost tempted to say, 'I'm confused and worried because I don't know what you're thinking or feeling and whether this is a big thing for you or whether it's casual and I'm wondering what happens when we get back to London and whether we're in a relationship. Is that what this is?'

But she bit those words back.

'Freaking out?' he prompted.

'No,' she said firmly. 'I'm…' Worried, concerned, apprehensive…so maybe, yes, maybe freaking out a little.

'Usually when I don't know about a relationship, I come and talk to you,' she began.

Ben nodded.

'But in this case, it's tricky.'

'Because you want to talk about me.'

She nodded.

'You can still talk to me.'

'But…' No, she couldn't. There was no way she could give voice to all the questions circling in her head.

'How about I start?' he said. 'So, Charlotte, did you get lucky last night?'

It was the first time Ben had asked that question and actually wanted to hear the answer. She looked at him through narrowed eyes, then her face brightened as she realised what he was getting at.

'I did, as it happens.'

'Lucky you.' He couldn't suppress his smile.

'Yes, and lucky him.'

Ben laughed.

'Can I take it from your answer that the sex was good?'

'The sex was great.'

'Just great?'

She swatted him. 'You're fishing for compliments now.'

'No, I'm just trying to understand. Tell me about him? What's he like?'

'He's very good with his hands. But I shouldn't be surprised by that, he's an artist.'

Ben sat where he was, forcing himself not to go straight to her and climb on top of her on the day bed. She wanted to talk and it was so important that they kept talking.

'An artist? You need to watch out for them.'

She laughed.

'So the sex was phenomenal.' He steeled himself for the next question. 'But how do you feel about him?'

He held his breath, fearing that he'd gone too far.

'He's one of my favourite people in the world. So, there's that.'

'That's a good start, isn't it?'

'It's a great start. The best. But…'

Oh, God, this was it. *But I don't think I want a relationship with him. Or anyone.*

'But I'm not sure how he feels.'

Ben allowed himself to exhale. 'Ahh…'

'And we talk a lot about how I feel but we don't talk as much about how he feels. I'm worried he's holding something back. Or that he's not as interested. He seems unsure.'

Unsure? Him? That was not what he was expecting her to say.

'Well, from what you told me and relying on my knowledge of being a man, I would guess, and it's just a guess…'

'Of course.' Her lips curled into a delicious grin.

'I would guess that he feels the same way you do.'

There. He couldn't possibly know if that was the truth, because he wasn't sure how she was feeling about him.

But it wasn't a lie, exactly, he told himself.

'Would he, you know, from what you know as a man, have thought the sex was good?'

Ben leaned towards her. 'I'm pretty sure he thought the sex was phenomenal. Probably the best he's had in his life.'

A lovely blush spread across Charlotte's cheeks.

'And how do you think he feels, theoretically, about what's going on?'

'I'm pretty sure he feels the same way as you,' he repeated.

'But could you be more specific?'

She looked down at him, eyes full of uncertainty and questions.

He thinks he might love you.

The words in his head made him pull back and Charlotte mirrored his actions, startled, eyes wide.

He loved her. But that was the last thing he could tell her. She'd fly out of the door without a backward glance if he confessed that. But he had to say something, because she was sitting across from him now looking crestfallen.

'I think he's excited about the new developments in your relationship.'

She tilted her head. That answer wasn't good enough for her. But it was all he could say without frightening her.

'He's very excited. And happy. But he's also a little nervous, because you are so very important to him, and he doesn't want to stuff anything up between the two of you.'

'But he's excited? Pleased?'

'Very. Because you are also one of his favourite people in the world. And the sex was phenomenal.'

She laughed.

'And I think he'd like to show you again how good it can be. Just to put that question beyond doubt.'

'Oh.' Charlotte considered this. 'I think that would be okay.'

Ben moved back to her and his lips dropped to kiss her beautiful shoulder as he let his fingers stroke her silken arms. He felt her relax under his touch. Her lids lowered. She might not love him yet, but he would do everything within his power to make sure she did eventually. And if that meant holding back his true feelings for a little longer, then that was what he had to do.

Charlotte looked at her wardrobe.

She wanted to wear something that would wow him. An outfit that would make more than just his jaw drop, an outfit that would make him fall in love with her.

She sighed. She only had what was in her suitcase. It would have to be the green. A long cotton sundress, but with a fitted bodice and low neckline. She showered and dressed and scolded herself for being so wound up about this. If Ben were any other man, she'd be relaxed. Nonchalant even.

But he wasn't just any man, he was her Ben. Their conversation earlier had been fun, and she supposed that she should be happy with everything he'd told her, but she couldn't shake the feeling that he was still holding something back. He'd agreed the sex had been phenomenal.

Probably the best he'd had in his life.

That should be enough for now, shouldn't it?

Part of her knew that she shouldn't push things, but the other part of her felt as if she were in limbo. Not knowing if they were moving forward or back or anything. Not knowing if he thought this would last when they got back to London.

Ben's relationship track record was as sparse as hers. He also never lasted beyond a few dates.

Was that what he thought would happen between him and Charlotte?

She wanted him to like her. She wanted him to love her.

She walked out of her room and waited for Ben to turn around. Her palms were damp, whether from the humidity or nerves. She wiped them on her dress. At the rate she was going the dress would be soaked by the evening's end.

Ben turned and smiled. For a moment she forgot her mission and could only look at him. He was wearing a soft shirt, open at the neck, and loose trousers. His hair was washed and he'd shaved. She bit her lip and considered simply undressing him there and then, and forgetting about dinner. He stepped up to her, eyes wide. 'Charlotte, you look amazing.' He brushed his lips against her cheek and she felt her knees weaken.

'Shall we?' he asked. 'The sooner we get there, the sooner we can get back.'

That sounded like very good logic to Charlotte.

They held hands as they walked, but he let go as soon as they approached the restaurant. It disappointed her, but she told herself it was okay, he wasn't ready to announce the changed nature of their relationship to the world. It was sensible even. But for once, she wished Ben was not so utterly sensible.

'Is everything okay?' he asked, as if he could read her thoughts.

'It's fine. No, great!' She forced a lightness into her tone.

'I'm sorry we have to do this.'

'No, don't be sorry. This is why we came. Why I came. It'll be a good night.'

Ben looked at her as if he didn't believe her and motioned for her to enter the restaurant first.

So much for wooing Ben and getting him to open up more. Tonight Charlotte was at the quiet end of the table. She was seated next to Ben's aunt and Gus's brother, who seemed considerably older than Gus and nowhere near as charming. Ben was at the other end of the table with a group of younger people, including a couple and their two young children. Ben's cousins. Charlotte was not great at guessing children's ages, but one of the children, with a mop of messy brown curls, was toddling around and chatting to people. The other was being passed between its parents' laps.

When the food arrived in front of them, Ben stood. Was he leaving? Giving a speech? What was he doing?

Ben reached down and said something to the child's mother. She smiled and then passed the baby to Ben, who held it and rocked it while the child's parents ate their dinner.

He knew how to hold a baby. When on earth did he learn that?

Watching Ben hold the baby did very strange things to Charlotte's insides.

I just must be hungry, she thought, and loaded up her plate with more noodles.

Charlotte did not pay any attention to what the people around her were talking about, too busy watching the scene at the other end of the table. Once the baby was passed back to its mother, the toddler tugged Ben's sleeve and he lifted her onto his lap. Within moments Ben had the toddler laughing at something. Charlotte strained to hear what on earth he was saying. Not only was he comfortable holding the baby, but he also knew how to talk to them. She'd thought she knew Ben inside out, but now she felt as though she was getting to know him all over again. It was unsettling.

And wonderful.

Ben picked up her hand again once they were out of sight of the restaurant.

'Are you okay?' he asked.

'Yes, just tired.'

Back at the villa, she washed her face and brushed her teeth. Ben gave her a sheepish grin. 'So, I've run out of condoms. I thought I had more, but I clearly did not anticipate I'd be needing so many. Do you happen to have any more?'

Clearly sleeping with her had not been on Ben's radar at all. If she hadn't thrown herself at him then it wouldn't have crossed his mind.

What was she going to do with all these feelings that were getting stronger every day and pulling her towards Ben?

Charlotte held her stomach. It felt empty. Which was strange given she'd eaten half a Balinese feast at dinner.

She didn't want the condom. She didn't even want her IUD.

For the first time in her life the thought of getting pregnant didn't terrify her. The idea of a baby growing inside her, of *Ben's* baby growing inside her, didn't scare her—in fact she craved it. A baby that would grow up into a little child like the one he'd been talking to at dinner, with a mop of light brown curly hair on its head and his big blue eyes.

She clutched her stomach tighter. Now that the image was planted in her mind, she couldn't shake it. Kids were not on her agenda; they were on a five-year planner that hadn't even been printed yet.

She wanted Ben's babies.

And it was terrifying. She wanted to wake up to Ben's smiling face looking at her when she woke up every morning.

And Ben still thought they were friends. Ben who didn't want to hold her hand in front of his family.

'Actually, I want to go for a walk,' she said.

'A walk? The chemist will be shut.'

'No, yes, not for that. I just need a walk.'

'Okay, I'll get my shoes.'

'You don't need to come,' she snapped more forcefully than she'd intended.

Ben didn't blink. If anything, he became calmer. He was still as he said, 'I'm not letting you walk around in the dark alone.'

'Fine, come,' she said. It was the only way of not having to explain the excess energy rising inside her and her sudden need to get out of the villa where they had spent most of the day making love.

Being with Ben negated the whole purpose of the walk, which was to get away from him, to have some time to think and process what was going on in her head. And her stomach. And her heart.

There were no streetlights and, once they'd passed the cluster of hotels and villas near them, only the occasional house. She grudgingly admitted to herself that Ben was right, she didn't want to be walking alone. While the island felt safe, it was still an unfamiliar place.

'When did you get so good at kids?' she asked.

He laughed. 'I wouldn't say I'm an expert.'

'But with those kids at dinner?'

'My cousin May's kids? The toddler is Isabelle. The last time I saw her was at Dad's funeral last year. She was only just walking then. And the baby is Teddy.'

Isabelle and Teddy. Lovely names. What would

they call their kids if they ever had them? She'd always liked Jacob. And Emilia.

'You were good with them. You knew what to do.'

'Hardly. I know that parents need to eat. And need every break they can get.'

'So, you don't want kids?' Charlotte froze. She couldn't believe she'd just asked that.

She couldn't believe she didn't know. They'd known one another for years, but never discussed this. If only she'd asked him this question three weeks ago when nothing was hanging on it.

'I…ah…' Ben stopped walking.

'You don't.'

'Char, I never… That is, I don't know.' A taxi truck drove past and its headlights crossed Ben's face. She could see the look of shock on it.

'I don't mean with me, I mean, just generally. In theory,' she clarified.

'I guess, one day, I suppose so,' he said.

He supposed so. As if he were doing her some sort of favour.

'Fine!' she barked, declaring that everything really was *not* fine.

'Charlotte, what's going on? What's the matter?'

She couldn't tell him. She couldn't tell him about everything that was whirling around inside her. New feelings, new desires. Some of the desires were so unexpected and so powerful she was overwhelmed by them.

Ben, I think I want to have your babies and it terrifies me.

She turned away and took some steadying breaths. Ben hadn't said he didn't want kids, he was giving her a perfectly rational and calm answer to her questions. They'd slept together for the first time less than forty-eight hours ago and she was now expecting him to say that they would have babies together?

She wasn't all right. She was confused. Shaken.

But he was so unruffled, as if this wasn't affecting him at all.

She tried to study his face in the almost dark. 'How are you not freaking out?'

'What do you mean?'

'I mean…' She waved her hands around hoping he would understand without her having to spell it out. 'I mean, about this. Us. You're so calm. Don't you care?'

Ben walked over to her, slowly. Still so bloody calm.

'I'm not calm.'

'You look calm. You seem positively bored.'

'Bored!'

'Yes, bored, as if you sleep with your best friend every day.'

In the darkness, his hands found hers. 'I am freaking out,' he said. 'I'm just internalising my freak-out.'

'But you are freaking out?'

'Totally. I'm panicking and excited and…and I'm trying to appear calm so you don't panic.'

Could that be it? Ben was more sensible than her, in some ways. He had the neat apartment, he was always on time. But she sometimes had to remind him how to get where they were going. Together, they always managed to figure things out.

And they would now. She squeezed his hand.

'Is that true? Are you really freaking out on the inside?'

He nodded. 'Like a duck in a pond. Calm on the surface, paddling like a mad thing below.'

'What are we going to do?' She needed to know how to handle these feelings, whether she should be holding something back or letting herself fall entirely and irretrievably.

'Take each day as it comes. Is there anything else?'

'It might help me if I can see you freaking out a bit more?'

'How would that possibly help?'

'I don't know, but I'd feel less crazy.'

He pulled her against him. He kissed behind her ears, down her neck. A warm feeling began to fill her belly.

'Paddling madly?' she asked.

'Madly. Frantically,' he murmured tenderly into her neck.

'So am I.'

CHAPTER NINE

BEN LAY ON his back in Charlotte's bed and she curled against him. She held his hand and was twirling her fingers through his. To an outsider it might have looked like a dreamy scene, but Charlotte was on edge. Oh, she might not have been on the brink of leaving the island and going back to London, but she was giving him sideways glances and screwing up her face with worry when she thought he wasn't looking. He had to remain steady for both their sakes.

They had shared their most honest conversation so far, but underlying it all he sensed she was worried about her feelings and about hurting his. She was worried about the future.

He wanted a future with Charlotte. He wanted to give himself to her body and soul for the rest of his life.

He didn't know where this new path would take them, but the last thing he wanted was Charlotte out of his life, so he had to take things slowly if things were going to have a chance of working out between them.

'What are we going to do today?' he asked.

'Stay here?' she answered.

It was so tempting. After all, they had everything they needed. A pool to lie beside, food to be delivered. Each other. They could, he rationalised, stay here for ever.

But this was Bali! On the other side of the world. A long London winter lay ahead of them and there would be plenty of time to cuddle up in bed during the next few months.

He was getting ahead of himself. They had discussed the fact that they were both excited but nervous, but neither of them had broached the subject of what would happen back in London. Would they be able to keep their new relationship alive? Or would it die out slowly? Or worse, end quickly. Dramatically. Irretrievably.

Just because he wanted to spend all day in bed with her, that didn't mean that was what they should do. They were friends first and foremost and he was trying not to forget that important fact. They should do something that friends would do. They had to preserve that part of their relationship.

'That would be nice,' he replied.

'You left off the "but".'

'Don't you think we should make the most of our time here?'

'I thought we were?' The smile that broke over her face made him tingle all over. He was about to roll over and pull her to him, but he held firm.

'I think we should make the most of our last couple of days. The wedding is tomorrow and we leave the day after that. There's still a lot we haven't seen.'

If he didn't get out of bed, they would make love again and, yes, it would be wonderful, but every time they made love, he felt a little closer to her. Fell a little more.

She sighed. 'You're right. We should explore. Where would you like to go? Swimming? Surfing?'

'Gus said we should really visit Nusa Ceningan. It's the next island over and there's a famous yellow bridge between the two. Nusa Ceningan is meant to have beautiful beaches. Romantic.' As soon as the words slipped out, he wanted them back. So much for not spooking Charlotte.

But to his delight, her face lit up. 'Let's do it.'

Ben was holding back.

Oh, not in bed. In bed he was very much on board with what was happening. But he was still holding something back.

Just because you're friends and you have sex, that doesn't mean this is a relationship, she reminded herself.

Except that he'd suggested a romantic island visit. That was what he'd said, wasn't it?

Ben had pulled his phone out and was scrolling through his emails as though he hadn't just dropped the R word.

At what point did 'friends who had sex' become something more? At what point were they in a relationship? If only he'd give her a sign that this was more than just a two-friends-having-sex arrangement.

He'd told her that he was panicking too but, given the infuriatingly calm way in which he seemed to be approaching this, she assumed that was largely for her benefit. Besides, he'd also told her repeatedly that their friendship was the most important thing, the thing they had to protect above all else.

She knew—logically—that she had to give their relationship time to evolve. They were on the other side of the world, away from their real lives, and neither of them could predict what might happen when they returned to London.

In the meantime, they were going to a romantic beach.

She climbed out of bed, naked in the daylight. Ben looked at her appreciatively and she felt herself blush. It was a lot to get used to, seeing one another naked. Though, she was convinced, a thoroughly positive change in their relationship.

She ran a finger down his bare foot, sticking out over the edge of the bed, tickling him. 'Let's go see these beaches.'

After breakfast and dressing they walked out of the villa and to the concierge that operated the accommodation to find a means of getting to the island.

'Where are you off to?' the assistant asked.

'Nusa Ceningan.'

She shook her head. 'There are no cars allowed on Nusa Ceningan either. But you can rent scooters,' she said, pointing to a row of small motorcycles.

'We could walk,' Charlotte suggested.

'No, it's too far. And too hot. Take a scooter,' the woman insisted.

'Change of plan,' Ben said. 'We'll find a closer beach.'

But Nusa Ceningan was *romantic*. He wanted to go. And she did too.

Charlotte stared at the scooters. They weren't actual motorbikes. Not exactly like Tim had been riding. More like mopeds.

'We don't have to go,' Ben said softly.

'But you want to.'

'Not this much. Charlotte, it's okay.'

'Just give me a moment.'

It wasn't her preferred mode of transport, but they wouldn't travel fast.

Ben stood still and Charlotte went to the bike.

At university, she had ridden a bicycle everywhere. Tim had as well. One the paths, on the roads. In London owning a car was impractical, not to mention expensive, so Tim had decided a motorcycle was the mode of transport for him. Charlotte had thought him lazy, more than anything else, as she preferred walking and the Tube, and it hadn't occurred to her that a motorbike would be dangerous.

Tim was a good rider, and for nearly two years he rode the motorbike without incident. But even the best riders could face trouble in cold, icy rain. It was always the rain that had worried her most, slippery, blinding, and unpredictable.

She knew she didn't have to do this. She and Ben could turn around and walk to a nearby beach. Or go back to the villa and bed.

But she didn't want to be stuck any more. She was tired of being scared and Ben wanted to do this.

Romantic.

She walked up to the scooter and placed her hand on the seat, as if touching it would answer her question. The leather seat was warm from the sun. She nodded.

Ben didn't say anything but raised his brows to confirm.

'Yes, I'd like to do this.'

'You can share, you know?' said the woman.

Ben and Charlotte looked at one another. Cosying up on a bike behind Ben? Where could she sign up? She nodded.

'You trust me?' he asked.

'Of course I do.' *With my life.*

They did the paperwork and the woman offered to show them how to ride. It was a relatively simple matter of turning the key and accelerating or braking. Balancing was easier than on a bicycle, not that she'd ridden one of those in years either.

'Helmets?' Ben asked and the woman handed them two.

Once their helmets were on, they got on the scooter, Ben first and Charlotte behind.

'Just yell if I'm going too fast or if you want me to stop.'

'I will, but I'll be fine.'

Ben looked even more worried than she felt as he turned forward and started the scooter. He drove slowly onto the road. ·

The road was smooth at first, but as they made their way across the island the more potholes they came across and the rougher the road became. She didn't feel worried, but she did have to concentrate on holding onto Ben. Though it was hardly a problem. Holding onto Ben was her new obsession. After a while, Ben pulled over to the side of the road.

'Is everything okay?' she asked.

'Yes, I just wanted to check how you're doing.'

'I'm fine. It's actually fun.'

Ben smiled, but only with his mouth. She reached over and rubbed his arm reassuringly. 'Really, it's fun. I'm glad we're doing this.'

'The yellow bridge isn't too much further.'

Charlotte got used to the rhythm of the scooter accelerating, braking, and taking the corners gently.

She let go, not just of fears and worry about her safety. Or Tim. But also, her fears and worry about her future with Ben. After a while she stopped concentrating on the bike and began to notice everything else around her—the rush of the green scenery running past, the feel of the sun on her hands, the air brushing her face. In the humidity it could hardly be called a breeze, but it wasn't unpleasant. Most of all, she focused on the way Ben's back felt against her cheek. The way the muscles in his arms and legs looked as he steered and manoeuvred the bike. The world looked different from the back of a scooter, but maybe she was just looking at the world differently.

The yellow bridge was a narrow suspension bridge spanning the waterway between the two islands of Nusa Lembongan and Nusa Ceningan. It was made of wood and slightly rickety, reminding her of one of the suspension bridges over deep canyons in movies, only the bridge was low and crossed a strait of clear blue water.

There was a queue to cross the bridge, with only a certain number of people and bikes allowed at a time and traffic from both sides taking turns to cross. The crossing was also slowed down by tourists stopping halfway for photos of the beautiful view, taking in the seaweed farms and colourful fishing boats. But no one seemed to mind, no one was in a hurry. Not when they were all in such a beautiful, tranquil place.

Charlotte took out her phone and started taking some shots as well.

'Smile!' She caught Ben's handsome face by surprise.

She had plenty of photos of Ben, but that was Bearded Ben. Friend Ben. This Ben—her Ben—was different. This photo would be different.

'And a selfie.'

He stood dutifully next to her, wrapping his arms around her and standing close. She moved in even closer, their cheeks touching. Sparks shot down her arm, causing her hand to tremble slightly. Charlotte angled to get the bridge in behind them and just as she was lining up another shot, Ben glanced away from the camera and towards her. As Charlotte hit the button Ben was looking directly at her. And smiling.

He stepped away and when Charlotte regarded the photo her stomach swooped. Anyone looking at this photo would see two people who were more than a little comfortable with one another's bodies. Tanned faces, close cheeks, bright eyes, bodies wrapped around one another's. She even fancied, for the briefest of moments, that her camera had captured a look of desire crossing Ben's face.

She'd look at these later and they would either make her happy or crush her.

Depending on what happened next.

'Are you going to post those?' he asked with a guarded voice, as though he'd read her thoughts.

If you post these, people will speculate that we're more than friends.

She had last posted a picture of them supping champagne in the airport lounge and another from the craft shops in Ubud, but apart from that she hadn't posted any photos of the trip to social media.

The highlights of the trip had all been decidedly not for general viewing.

She shook her head.

If Ben wasn't ready to announce their new-found intimacy to the word, then neither was she.

While they waited to cross, Charlotte looked up the history of the bridge.

'Did you know it's also called the Bridge of Love?'

Annoyingly Ben had put on his sunglasses and she couldn't read his expression as he said, 'No, I didn't know that.'

The Bridge of Love. That was his opportunity to use that word.

Throw it out there. See how it felt, how it sounded on his lips.

Love.

But he didn't.

Of course he didn't. This was commitment-phobe Ben. Two-date Ben.

They were, as everyone said, firm members of CA: Commitment-phobes Anonymous.

If you're not going to use that word, why are you expecting Ben to?

Ben might not have used the L-word but he did keep looking from the scooter to her with concern, so she smiled broadly. 'I'm okay. I'm having a good time,' she insisted. As she spoke, she realised it was the truth. No exaggeration was necessary; she was having a great time. The scooter wasn't fast, there wasn't much other traffic and it had brought them here, to this beautiful spot and this charming bridge.

They crossed the bridge, stopping with everyone else in the centre for more photos before continuing on to the island and the beach Ben wanted to visit.

Like all the other beaches in the vicinity, it was picturesque, with clear turquoise water and small waves that lapped gently up the white sands. The beach, like a few across the islands, had a swing. Not a large rope swing for daredevils to launch themselves into a lake or river, but a swing like at a children's playground, where people could sit and swing, dipping their toes in the water. This one had a double swing and was shaded by a broad umbrella. One swing each.

Romantic.

They bought some cool drinks from a nearby cafe and returned to the beach.

He handed her one of the drinks and said, 'You want to try the swing, don't you?'

She nodded. 'Don't you?'

Luckily the swing was unoccupied and they both claimed their seats. It had been years since Charlotte had swung on a swing, and the sensation of swooping in her stomach from the lifting and falling was a lot like what her body had been through the past few days with Ben.

It really was romantic. Clear blue, clean, amazing water, swinging, feet dragging through the water.

She laughed.

Ben turned to her and spoke earnestly. 'Are you having a good time?'

'Of course. I'm having a great time.'

'Thank you for coming.'

She shook her head. 'No, thank you for bringing me.'

Not having come to Bali with Ben was inconceivable. This week had changed her life. She just wasn't sure yet how much.

They passed Will and Summer on their return to the village, Charlotte still filled with endorphins after her ride. She felt energised by the exercise, but something else as well. By overcoming her fear of riding she'd unblocked something that had been holding her back. Ben was beside her, beaming, and she felt on top of the world. She greeted them both warmly and Summer gave her a hug.

'We've just ridden to the yellow bridge. It was great,' Charlotte enthused.

'We're just about to go surfing. Do you want to come?'

Charlotte looked to Ben and his eyes were wide. Charlotte had hoped they would go straight back to the villa, but she knew Ben loved to surf. At least he had once. He'd told her several times that it was one of the things he missed most about Australia.

'Ben?'

Ben looked to his brother and back to Summer. Charlotte, not caring what the others might read into the gesture, rubbed Ben's arm. 'You want to, don't you?'

Ben nodded. 'But do you?'

'I don't have to surf. But I'd like to watch,' she said low and suggestive, so only Ben could hear.

He straightened his spine and nodded. 'Sounds great. Just let us get our things.'

The four of them headed off to the famous surf beach at the northern end of the island. Charlotte was relaxed, and finally felt Ben was too. He was chatting away happily with Will about what they all might do that evening. Diane and Gus were having a quiet night alone as it was the evening before the wedding, and Summer suggested the four of them have an early dinner, to which Ben quickly and surprisingly agreed.

Maybe his attitude to Will was thawing.

Charlotte wasn't sure why it bothered her that the brothers didn't get along, but it did. Having no siblings of her own, she had always envied those who had them. It seemed like too important a relationship to toss aside capriciously.

Will hurt him.

Maybe, though Charlotte wasn't exactly sure why, Ben blamed Will for the actions of their father. Charlotte doubted that Will told his father not to pay Ben's university tuition. Or to refuse to extend the same perks that Will received.

Still, she didn't know everything that had gone on in the Watson household and had promised Ben she would not meddle.

Charlotte had dressed in her swimsuit, but felt she had exhausted quite enough courage and adrenaline for the day. Besides, the view was far better from the beach. It was hard to suppress the smile from her face as she watched Ben carry his board into the surf, his muscles rippling under his bronzed skin as he paddled out. She pressed her lips together as she watched his lean, strong body balance on the board as he rode a short wave in.

This was, she was quite convinced, paradise.

Charlotte stretched out on the beach and let the sun soak into her skin. Two more sleeps till they went home. Two more nights sharing the villa with Ben. Her body still thrummed from the night before. Summer was right, it was better just to see what happened and take each day at a time and not think too far ahead. She had to keep reminding herself that planning your life out perfectly was often a waste of time as too many unpredictable things would always be thrown your way. Charlotte knew that better than most.

Ben was more relaxed today as well. After speaking last night, she'd realised that his hesitation wasn't due to a lack of desire or interest, only caution and a wish not to see the friendship unravel.

But right now, she pushed the future from her mind. She watched Ben, in the shallows with Will, both of them showing Summer how to surf. Charlotte couldn't help but smile. She liked seeing the brothers getting along cooperating, not competing.

She closed her eyes and let her body relax, remembering how it had felt when Ben's fingers had stroked her the night before. She felt so alive with him, yet so comfortable. A strange mix of excitement and security.

She must have been dozing when a sound to her side shook her from her daydreams. She sat up, rubbing her eyes.

'Sorry to wake you,' Will said, rummaging in his bag.

Charlotte stretched. 'You didn't wake me. I was just being lazy.'

Will picked up his phone and moved a few metres away. It looked like he was making some kind of work-related call. Charlotte shook her head. She wondered how Summer coped with Will's workaholic tendencies. She and Ben at least had the same amount of drive and ambition. They could both get lost in their work and, particularly before a big exhibition, it could become all-consuming for both. But they also knew how to wind down and experience the other joys in life.

Ben and I are well matched.

She shook the thought away again. She was meant to be taking things one day at a time, not thinking too far into the future.

She looked out at the waves and spotted Ben and Summer moving into the water. Ben holding his board confidently and surely. Summer with a smaller board. Ben managed to climb on first and began to paddle.

Charlotte knew in theory that Ben had spent much of his childhood at the beach swimming and surfing, though she'd never quite imagined the scene before her now, watching him, with his broad shoulders and tanned chest, navigating the waves as if he'd done it all his life. Summer was less certain and, unlike the brothers, she'd avoided the more challenging waves. But she climbed onto her board now, lay on her stomach and followed Ben.

There were so many things about Ben that Charlotte was only just discovering. He was a revelation. Ben and Summer moved further out, both of them deftly navigating the waves.

She watched Ben climb onto the board, then his knees, and catch a superb wave. The look on his face was priceless. It was worth travelling halfway around the world to see him look so happy and fulfilled.

It was worth travelling around the world for many other reasons too, she reflected.

Charlotte's eyes didn't travel far from Ben so, like him, she didn't see the giant wave until it was already on top of him.

The wave crashed over the boards and Charlotte lost sight of them both.

CHAPTER TEN

CRAP.

That was Ben's overwhelming thought as the wave loomed over him and Summer. He saw her on her board a few metres to his left.

'Breathe!' he yelled to her with his last breath, the instant before the wave came down on them with the force of a collapsing brick wall.

The water pushed Ben under and he felt himself being washed around, water swirling and tossing him everywhere at once. He tried surfacing but was pushed down again. Just when he thought he was out of breath his face hit the air and it filled his lungs before he was sucked down and back into the churn again. He held onto his board for as long as he could, but his fingers were no match for the sea. It slipped from his fingers and the tug from the ankle rope pulled him further down. Or up. He could no longer tell.

Then, mercifully—or dangerously, he wasn't yet sure—he felt the rope go slack. He'd lost his board, but free from its drag he managed to get properly to the surface.

The first thing he did when he could see was look around for Summer, but she was nowhere. The high swell blocked his view in every direction. He couldn't even see the shore and, momentarily disoriented, didn't know which way to swim.

But his priority wasn't getting to the shore, it was finding Summer and making sure she was all right. Summer was a fair swimmer, but not as strong as him and Ben knew he was lucky to come through the wave that had just hit them. Summer, he feared, was out of her depth. Literally.

He looked around, but still couldn't see her. Panic slowly rose in his chest as each second passed without sight of her. He spun and spun. Seconds felt as though they were dragging out to minutes.

And then there she was. A flash of black and red in the blue. He yelled to her, but she didn't answer. He paddled towards her, but her body dipped beneath the surface again.

It only took a few seconds to reach her, but they were some of the longest of his life. He pulled her to the surface, twisting her so her face was out of the water. God knew where their boards were; his ankle stung where the cord had pulled and pulled before snapping. Summer's eyes were closed and her body limp and heavy. He tried to feel around her head for signs of an injury, but his arms were near dead with exhaustion. He turned onto his back, holding her to his chest and keeping her face and air passages out of the water. He didn't know if he could tread water like this for long, let alone swim back to shore, but he had no idea if anyone had seen the wave, or noticed them get swamped. He didn't have a spare hand to wave, so he turned his back to the beach and attempted a slow kick back.

He had to get there as soon as possible to get her breathing. There was no way he could attempt resuscitation here; he was barely keeping her face out of the choppy water. He kicked and kicked and shook her gently. 'Breathe, breathe,' he pleaded.

It was a dinghy that found them, washing small waves over them at first and, finally, two big arms reached into the water and hauled Summer, still lifeless, out of the water.

'Is she okay?' Ben asked the man piloting the boat, but he only shrugged.

As they approached the beach Ben looked at Summer, still lifeless, and he swallowed back vomit.

On the beach, his legs were like jelly. He shook as though it were three degrees instead of thirty. Someone covered him with a towel, but he could barely feel it.

A paramedic came over to assist him, but Ben wouldn't answer until he was assured that Summer was, indeed, breathing. They assured him she was and Ben almost cried with relief. They asked him some questions about what had happened with Summer and how long she had been underwater for, how long she was unconscious. Ben wasn't sure, but gave him his best guess as somewhere between ten seconds and a minute.

He looked around for Charlotte but found Will standing next to him. Ben couldn't meet his eyes. He was meant to be watching Summer, teaching her. Not letting her get swamped by giant waves. Will must hate him more than ever.

'We're taking her to the medical centre. Do you need a lift there?' Will asked gruffly.

Ben shook his head. 'No, I'll just go back to the villa.'

'Are you sure? I think you should get yourself checked out.'

Do you?

Ben held back his petulant response. The last thing he needed now was Will trying to play parent.

Will touched Ben's shoulder and turned him to face him. Ben was about to shake off his brother's hand and ask what he thought he was doing when he saw Will's eyes. They weren't angry. Or annoyed. They were brimming with tears. Before Ben knew what was going on Will had dragged him into a tight hug.

Ben could smell the sweat and worry on his

brother. 'Thank you,' Will choked. 'Thank you for being there. Thank you for saving her.'

Ben was too stunned to respond before Will released him, turning back to Summer.

Charlotte held Summer's hand as the paramedics explained that Summer would be all right, but they wanted her to get looked over at the medical centre and determine whether she needed to go to the main island to be checked.

Summer spoke slowly but clearly, and told them she felt fine. Just shaken.

'We're not taking any chances,' Charlotte said.

Summer was helped to a sitting position and Charlotte looked around for Will, but she couldn't see either Watson brother.

Her heart still pounded, so she sucked in a deep breath and then another and several more in quick succession before she noticed that none of the air seem to be getting to her brain. Will suddenly appeared and took her shoulders, turning her to face him. 'Charlotte, are you okay?'

She nodded, but she was still gasping.

'Charlotte, Charlotte, look at me.'

She found Will's eyes but they were grey, a dull and substandard version of Ben's.

'Now, breathe when I say. Can you do that?'

She nodded, still gasping.

'In,' he said. 'Hold it, now slowly out. Wait. Wait. Now, in again, slowly. And hold.'

She did as she was told, slowly exhaling, holding her breath and the gasping stopped, but she didn't feel any better. She felt as though she might throw up.

'Everything's okay, they're both in and safe. They're going to be all right. Everything's okay,' he repeated.

Ben and Summer might be on shore safely, but everything was most definitely not okay.

Once he was satisfied that Charlotte was still breathing, Will's attention went elsewhere. He scooped up Summer's things and said, 'They're taking her to the medical centre as a precaution.'

Charlotte nodded. She should be the strong one now, not collapsing in a hyperventilating mess. She needed to be there for Summer and Will. And Ben.

But she was having a hard enough time holding herself together.

'Call us,' she said to Will as he went to Summer without a backward glance.

It was over, they would be okay. Summer was breathing, probably a little bruised, but she would be fine.

Her eyes finally landed on Ben, standing a few metres away from her on the beach. His beautiful face was crestfallen. His perfect shoulders slumped. She rushed to him and threw her arms around him.

'She's okay, you're okay. Thank goodness.'

Ben was shaking. She hugged him tighter, but the shakes were almost violent and she couldn't still them.

She didn't think she could do this. She didn't know how to deal with Ben's shock when she was barely in control of her own.

The wave had swamped them. Knocked them both under and sideways and she hardly knew what. She'd lost sight of him for ages. She didn't know how long it was in actual seconds, but it was long enough for the fear to travel from her brain, down her spine and to take hold, hard and heavy. Long enough that she'd had time to worry about how on earth she would feel arriving back at Heathrow alone.

And that was long enough.

She should feel delighted that he and Summer were both all right, but now that the fear had taken hold in her heart, she couldn't shift it.

'Do you want to go to the medical centre?' she asked Ben.

He shook his head. 'I just want to go to the villa. Then check on Summer.'

'She's conscious. She's going to be all right. Thanks to you.'

'I should have seen the wave.'

'Ben, no one saw the wave! No one could have got out of the way quickly enough.'

Ben frowned. 'I was teaching her. I should have been paying better attention.'

Charlotte reached out her hand to take his, but something about the way he was holding himself, made her take her hand back.

They walked slowly back to the villa, neither of them speaking, both studying the people and the scenery as they went past. So much had changed since this morning. And not in a good way.

They showered and, after, Charlotte considered her available outfits. She guessed, without being told, that dinner with Will and Summer was no longer on the evening's agenda and she was relieved. She wasn't in the mood to socialise. She wanted a light dinner. Maybe a glass of wine and then to find something mindless on the television to fall asleep to.

And she wanted to do those things alone.

She needed to.

Ben was in her head and her heart. He was in her chest. Running through her veins. And she couldn't think properly when he was near. He was messing with her navigation system, like a magnet on a compass. And now, especially, she needed to think straight.

She chose loose cotton trousers and a T-shirt and put those on, then went, with trepidation, to speak to Ben.

He was by the pool, hunched over his phone. Oblivious to the amazing sunset that was happening over the water right in front of him. To be honest, the sunset left Charlotte a little cool as well, compared to the forces running through her.

'I'm guessing dinner with Will and Summer is off?'

'Will just messaged. Summer's going to be fine, but they've told her to rest.'

Charlotte nodded.

'We could go out. Unless…' He looked her up and down. She was not dressed for a night on the town. Even in Bali.

'I'm exhausted too, I think I'd like to stay in.'

'Sounds perfect. We can order in.' He stood and moved towards her, taking her in his arms and pulling her to him, but as her cheek rested against his collarbone Charlotte stiffened. He was dressed now, dry, and no longer shaking, but the feeling of hugging him on the beach flashed back into her mind. Both of them shaking. Terrified.

When she froze, Ben did too. He pulled back slowly and she stepped away, looked at the floor.

'Char?' His voice was questioning, because he knew her so well. As well as she knew herself. Maybe even better because he knew exactly what she was about to say, even while she was still trying to find the words to say it.

She wasn't ready to lose someone else. She wasn't ready at all. She looked at her toes.

'Ben, I need a bit of time.'

'Time?'

'It's a lot.'

'What? Ordering dinner?'

'No. Everything. Us.'

She only looked at him once she'd said it. He nodded. As if he, annoyingly, understood. Maybe he could explain it to her, why she was suddenly feeling suffocated. Overwhelmed. Needing to flee. So she said what she knew, the part she did understand.

'I don't want to lose you,' she explained.

'You're not going to lose me.'

Charlotte shook her head. 'You can't promise that.'

She was going to lose him somehow. Maybe not to a wave, more likely because he didn't feel the same way about her.

'I can try. That's all anyone can ever do. I know you're upset about Tim—'

'No, I'm not. It's not that.' She'd ridden the scooter. She'd orgasmed with Ben, many times now. She'd let herself fall, finally, fall with abandon, gloriously. And hard.

It wasn't about *Tim*.

It was about fear. Fear that she would lose Ben just as she had lost Tim and the knowledge of just how much that would hurt.

'Do you want to…break up?'

'I don't know.'

The sound of those words sucked all the air from the space and surprised even Charlotte. She didn't want to break up with Ben, but she didn't know how she could do *this*.

'I don't know,' she scrambled. 'I know I need space. I need time. And I need to be alone.'

Ben's Adam's apple bobbed with a hard swallow. He blinked, didn't look at her. 'I understand.'

His reasonableness didn't make things easier, but it did make them smoother.

'Do you want me to leave?' she asked.

'Leave? Now?'

'Well, yes.'

'Of course not.'

'Given the circumstances—'

'What circumstances? It's seven at night, the evening before my mother's wedding, neither of us are leaving.'

'But I need space. I need to think. I could find another hotel.'

'Charlotte, no. Unless you would feel more comfortable?'

'Wouldn't you?'

He shook his head. 'I'll feel most comfortable knowing you're safe.'

'Ben…'

'I'm not going to stop caring about you.'

He was right, it was too late to run. It was too late to put a cork in her feelings—and his. She had to face them somehow. At some point.

Just not now. Not when, even though she seemed still, she was still shaking from the sight of the wave. She was still reeling from all the thoughts that had raced—no, stampeded—through her mind as Ben lay beneath the waves.

The difference between life and death was an instant.

'Can you please do me a favour?' he asked.

'What?'

'Don't leave. Please stay for the wedding.'

'I… I'm not sure that would be right. Wouldn't that be strange?'

'I think it would be stranger to come all this way and not go. Please don't change your flight. Stay here, I'll go somewhere else. I'll stay with Will. Just don't fly home yet.'

'Why not?' They could talk in London. Right now this villa was too small. This island was too small.

Though he was right, as much as she wanted space, she was exhausted and in no state to pack, get on a ferry to the mainland, let alone deal with the airline.

'I'll see in the morning. Ben, I just need space.'

Ben held up his hands. 'Take all you need.'

'Thank you for understanding.' She turned to go to her room and heard, 'Can you promise me we'll still be friends?'

She stopped mid-stride.

She needed time to think, and he was still wanting promises. Promises she didn't know she would be capable of keeping.

'I don't know. I honestly don't know.'

'Do you want to?'

Of course she wanted them to stay friends! And more. But as he kept saying, that wasn't the point.

'Friendship! You keep going on about friendship, like it's the most important thing.'

'But it is,' he pleaded.

'So that's all I am to you—a friend?'

'No, that's not all you are.' His eyes clouded over.

'But you think our friendship is the most important thing. You're so fixated on keeping our friendship that you're not even thinking of anything else.'

'That's not true.'

'It's exactly what you keep saying. Like a mantra. Like a broken record.'

His face reddened at her last words. Maybe she'd been a little blunt, but it was true.

'I'm just telling you that I don't want our friendship to end.'

She wanted to scream, release the hurt somehow. Because she saw now with perfect clarity that their friendship wasn't the most important thing to her. Their *relationship* was.

She certainly didn't want their friendship to end, but how could it continue when she loved him, and he didn't feel the same for her?

How could they go to gallery openings together and talk honestly about what they saw, while all the time she would want to be holding his hand? How could she go to his place for a cosy dinner when all she'd be able to think about was how she wanted to curl up in his bed? Feel him. Smell him. Touch him.

It hurt too much. Watching the wave take him out was bad enough, the bigger hurt would come every time they saw one another, and she'd be reminded that he didn't feel the same way she did.

If she hadn't known love with Tim, if she hadn't already experienced the crushing, ongoing, relentless pain of losing someone, then perhaps she could have been more casual with her heart. Perhaps she could continue to see Ben, casually, platonically. But she knew now she couldn't.

Losing Ben—either to a freak wave or to another woman—would be too much.

He didn't love her. Oh, he loved her as a friend, but he didn't feel the same uncontrollable passion that she felt for him. She had made the right decision.

'I hope we may be able to be friends again some time.'

'I don't understand. Are you saying you don't even want to be friends?'

'I'm saying I can't promise anything right now. That's what I've been trying to tell you.'

He dragged his hands through his hair and paced up and down the room. For a hotel it was spacious, but, still, it didn't allow him to take too many of his long powerful strides before he had to turn. The energy emanating from him felt explosive.

'I'm sorry, I think we need a break for a bit. I need a break and…' She motioned to him. 'I think you do too. I think we were too rash.'

'Rash? Charlotte, we've known one another for four years.'

'So? This week was…a lot.'

Ben closed his eyes and covered his face with his hands. A closed door would have had less effect.

Charlotte turned and moved to her room before either of them said something else, something there would be no coming back from.

Her room was empty without him. *She* was empty without him. She turned out the lights, drew the curtains, climbed into bed, and cried.

The sensation of a monster wave crashing over him was nothing—absolutely nothing—compared to how Ben felt now. Then he'd been flattened, half drowned, wind knocked out of him, water knocked into him. Disorientated. Shaken.

This was a hundred times worse.

Like the wave, it had been a surprise he hadn't seen coming. That morning, she'd ridden a scooter and he'd been so convinced it was a sign that she was managing to forget Tim.

She'd taken the selfie of them both and looked

on the verge of posting it online. A sure-fire way of announcing their relationship to the world.

She'd even used the L-word.

The Bridge of Love. The funny, quirky yellow bridge of love.

She couldn't tell him why it was called that, but he knew. Because it was where you came with the person you loved.

And he loved Charlotte.

For four long years he'd tucked it away, pushed it down. Ignored it. Because if he acknowledged the L-word he'd have to acknowledge how much he loved her, how deeply in love he was with Charlotte.

He'd refused to use the word when they first met.

Refused to think about it when they kissed.

He'd even refused to think about it when she'd pulled him into her the first wonderful time they had made love.

But now that word was suffocating him, drowning him, flattening him under its weight. Not to mention he no longer knew which way was up or down. He'd lost his only true compass— Charlotte—and he might never know the right way up again.

He loved her. He loved her with his entire heart.

Had they actually broken up? It was unclear, hence the sensation of still being tossed around in the powerful waves.

Well, he'd messed that up royally.

Done the thing he'd been trying not to do for the past four years—fall in love with Charlotte—and at the worst possible moment.

And to top it all off she'd denied their friendship was important.

No, she said it wasn't the most important thing.

Their friendship was everything. Solid, central.

No. You have another type of relationship. It's new. But it's there.

No, Charlotte didn't love him like that. She would have said. She wouldn't have asked for a break if she loved him.

It was that simple.

This moment felt inevitable. It was what he'd been worried about since Charlotte had first kissed him. It had been what he'd worried about since they'd first met! As soon as the relationship developed, Charlotte would run.

He took little comfort in the fact that she was still back at the villa and he was the one currently walking down the street looking for vacancy signs at the hotels.

She was probably booking her plane ticket.

He had to figure out what to tell his mother.

Charlotte won't be at the wedding after all... There was a family emergency.

They should get their story straight, but that would require communicating with one another and he wasn't sure that was allowed at the moment.

I need time. I need space.

Ben approached one of the open-air bars that were along the street. He should eat dinner, but the thought of food made his stomach tighten. But beer? He could do that.

He ordered and pulled out a stool with a view of the street, not wanting to look at the ocean after today's misadventure. The beer was cold and refreshing but he hardly tasted it.

CHAPTER ELEVEN

'HEY.'

Ben looked up and saw his brother. 'Hey.'

Will looked at Ben as though he could smell the stench of recent break-up. 'Where's Charlotte?'

'I'm not sure.' He wasn't. She might be on the ferry to Bali.

'You've lost her?'

'You could say that,' Ben mumbled.

Letting his brother's ambiguous comment slide, Will pulled up a stool. 'Can I join you?'

'Sure.'

The bartender approached and Will ordered a beer as well.

'I was just picking up some food for Summer,' he said. 'She loved the noodles we had here the other night and I thought I'd take them back to her. Mum's with her now.'

'That's nice of her. The night before the wedding.'

'She insisted on coming, needed to see for herself that Summer was all right.'

Will drank a third of the beer in one large gulp,

visibly relaxing as the alcohol spread through him. 'I'm glad I ran into you. I wanted to say thank you again.'

'For what?'

'What? For saving Summer. I'm so glad you were there.'

'I'm sorry I didn't see the wave coming.'

'No one saw the wave coming.'

Ben shook his head. He'd messed up so many things today. This was very un-Will-like behaviour, being grateful. Kind. But nothing could make Ben feel better at this point.

'So where is she? Really?' Will asked.

'I don't know. We had a…' Was it a fight? A disagreement?

A break-up.

'Whatever it was, shouldn't you go to her?' Will said.

'It's complicated.'

'So you say, but relationships are complicated. If they're not, then you're just acquaintances. And you and Charlotte are far more than mere acquaintances.'

'She's not over her ex.'

'Ex? When did they break up?'

'They didn't. Tim died.'

'Oh, I didn't know. When?'

'Seven years ago. Before we met. Motorbike accident.'

Will exhaled loudly.

'And you love her?'

This was businesslike Will back again. Straight down to the bare facts. Emotion be damned.

But Ben nodded.

'Did you tell her that?'

'No.'

'But you slept together?'

Ben bristled, but nodded again.

'And she said she wants to break up because she's not over her ex?'

'No.'

Will looked confused. 'Then what did she say exactly?'

'That she needed space. And some time to think.'

'Ahh.'

'You know I'm right.'

'No, you're not. That doesn't mean she's not over her ex, it means she needs space.'

Ben scrunched up his fists under the bar. Will saw things in black and white, like numbers, but Ben's world view was full of shades.

'I think she's over this guy. Seven years? I'd say so.'

'What would you know?' Ben regretted his tone, petulant and like the spoiled brat his father always accused him of being.

Will stared at him and for a moment Ben thought he was about to be on the receiving end of one of their father's lectures. Probably the one titled 'You need to work for your money'.

But Will's face broke and he laughed.

'The guy's been dead for years, she freaked out when she thought you had died. Give her a break—she's not upset because she's not over her ex, she's probably upset because she thought she was about to lose you, too.'

Ben shook his head. No. Charlotte would have told him that.

'If she felt anything like what I did this afternoon, she'd still be freaking out. I know you and Summer had a scary experience, but it was just as terrifying for those of us sitting on the beach.'

Ben regarded his brother, his face flushed, clearly relieved Summer was all right.

He almost believed what he was saying about Charlotte.

If she loved him, she wouldn't have let him leave.

Even if the wave did make her upset, it was only because it reminded her of Tim's accident.

Not because she loved Ben.

'You have two choices: you can spend the rest of your life being jealous of a dead guy. Or you can just go find her and tell her how you really feel.'

He couldn't do that. He'd always be second best. He'd always be runner-up to Tim.

'Don't you have to get back to Summer?' Ben said.

'Tim is gone,' Will said softly.

Tim hadn't gone. Tim was always around.

'I think she loves you. That's why she's freaked out. Do you think she'd behave like this or react like this if she didn't love you? She may not know that she loves you, but she definitely does.'

Will didn't know anything. Ben couldn't believe he'd even considered confiding in his brother.

Will finished the last gulp of his beer and stood. He then wrapped Ben into an unexpected bear hug. 'I've got to get back to Summer.'

Ben nodded, but as Will turned Ben said, 'Will, I've got a question. It's a bit out there. Please don't laugh.'

Will moved back to the stool but didn't sit.

'Did you buy my painting?'

Will looked sheepish and kicked the ground softly. 'It was a good investment.'

Ben knew his mouth was wide open but couldn't do anything to stop it. He was floored. Will was his mystery buyer.

'It wasn't then. Not ten years ago. Dad called it rubbish. I was an unknown artist. It was my first big sale.'

'I liked it. No, I love it. And I did then. It reminds me of when we were kids. At Middleton Beach.'

'Yes, that's it.' One of the beaches they'd swam and surfed at as kids.

'That sale paid for me to get to LA.'

'I'm not giving it back,' Will said.

'I don't…' Ben didn't want it back. Though it would be nice to see it again some time. 'That's not what I meant.'

He didn't know what he meant. Will had been the mystery buyer who had been prepared to drop ten grand on an unknown artist.

Will had had faith in him, before anyone else did.

'I'm proud of you,' Will said. 'It's a great painting. Everyone who comes into my office remarks on it.

Not only did he love Ben's painting, he displayed it in his office, where everyone could see it.

'You don't think I'm an irresponsible fool?'

'I'm not Dad. I'm in awe of your talent.'

Ben gave this a moment to sink in. Will wasn't his enemy. Will had simply been caught between Ben and their father.

'Why didn't you say anything?' It would have saved both of them a lot of pain.

'I wanted to tell you. I wanted you to know that I supported you. And that I thought you were brave and talented. And that I thought Dad was wrong.'

'You did?'

'Yes, Dad was brilliant in many ways, but when it came to you, he was…well, he wasn't always fair. He thought he was protecting you, but I could see you didn't want a bar of the business. It was always clear to anyone with an ounce of perspective that it wasn't you.' Will shifted from one foot to the other. 'I'd better get back to Summer with this food.'

Ben finished his beer then headed across the street to the hotel with the vacancy sign.

He had to give Charlotte space, if it was what she wanted. And spending the night in a different hotel was better than risking Charlotte getting on a plane. Maybe by the morning she'd be ready to talk, but for now he'd give her the space she needed. Even if his body was aching to be near her. He'd do anything for her, even this.

When Charlotte finally got through to someone at the airline it was only to be told that they could put her on a flight one day earlier, but it was going to cost her several thousand pounds. She thanked the person and ended the call. Was she really going to pay so much money to be a coward? No, she wasn't.

Her phone pinged with a message from Ben.

I've got a room at one of the hotels near the beach for the night so the villa is all yours.

Charlotte threw her phone down, fell back on the bed and screamed.

This was what she'd asked for, wasn't it? Space to think?

Or space not looking at Ben, feeling all these things for him and being terrified.

She took a bottle of white wine from the mini bar, went out to the patio, and poured a glass.

The view of the moonlight was spectacular, but, without Ben, the wine tasted of vinegar. She drank it anyway.

He's your best friend...are you really going to cut him from your life?

It was inevitable she would see Ben again. She couldn't avoid him altogether.

But if Ben didn't love her—body and soul—then she was lost. She couldn't continue their friendship without being honest with him about how she felt. And once she did that, she was certain to ruin their easy, uncomplicated camaraderie. He'd probably want to avoid her anyway...

Eventually, Charlotte fell into a restless sleep, waking regularly, remembering the day before and despairing again. Finally, in the early hours, exhaustion caught up with her and the next thing she knew she awoke to find the sun was high in the sky. She wandered out of her room. The villa was cool, despite the tropical weather—she could tell that Ben wasn't here and hadn't been here. She wandered out onto the patio.

The place didn't feel right without him.

She looked out of the window, across the bay to Bali. The sky was bright and clear and glorious, belying the turmoil inside her.

It was Diane and Gus's wedding day—in fact, the wedding was in a few hours—and she tried to imagine how Diane must be feeling. Excited? Nervous, maybe? Happy and relaxed, hopefully. Charlotte and Tim had only just started planning their wedding and hadn't even set a date.

Tim.

She wondered what he'd make of this mess she'd found herself in.

He'd tell you to pull yourself together.

She smiled. In the last weeks of his life, even when she was still hopeful that he'd overcome the wounds and infections that had ravaged his body, he'd made her promise she'd fall in love again. She'd promised that she would, but hadn't wanted to believe it would be a promise she'd have to keep. She'd still had hope.

She never gave much credence to a promise she'd made to placate Tim as he'd lain in pain.

He wanted you to move on. He'd say that you owe it to Ben to go to the wedding.

It was the whole reason she'd come to Bali after all: to support her best friend at his mother's wedding.

She wondered where Ben was. And she wondered how Summer was feeling.

Charlotte picked up her phone and sent a message to Summer.

Hey, there, how are you feeling this morning?

Her phone pinged soon after.

I'm doing so much better than yesterday. Still a little shaky but I had a good sleep.

Is there anything I can do?

Since you ask, I promised Diane I'd pick up her flowers. Could you possibly do it for me?

Charlotte wanted to say no. After all, she hadn't even decided if she was going to the wedding, if it would be right.

He's still your friend. He's still your best friend.

If she didn't go, they would all ask why and that would be awful for him.

Besides, it was Diane and Gus's day. She could hold herself together for a day if it meant not ruining someone else's wedding.

Charlotte messaged back.

For sure. What are the details?

'Charlotte, honey, what are you doing here?' Diane opened the door to her villa wearing a dressing gown. Her hair and make-up had been done and, even half dressed, she looked beautiful. Radiant.

'I've come to give you these.' She handed Diane the flowers. 'Summer asked me if I could.'

'Thank you, but, I mean, I thought you went home. Back to London?'

'What? No.'

'Ben said there'd been a family emergency.'

By the time Charlotte realised Ben had told his mother a white lie, Diane had as well. 'Is everything okay, or did my son just lie to his mother?'

'Um…everything… Um… I think he was just trying to protect me.'

'I think he was just trying to protect himself. Did you have a fight?'

'Not exactly. I was thinking of returning but I decided to stay. And come to the wedding, if that's still all right?'

Charlotte had worn her wedding outfit, the long blue dress she'd bought for the occasion. Physically, sartorially, she was ready to attend this wedding. Emotionally? She wasn't quite sure.

Diane studied her through narrowed eyes. 'Of course it is. I am glad you've stayed.'

Diane pulled Charlotte into an unexpected hug. 'Apart from anything else, Summer was supposed to help me zip up my dress. So you will have to do that.'

Charlotte sat and waited while Diane did the rest of her preparations. She took her gown out of its dust bag and Charlotte helped her into it, zipping up the back.

Diane looked stunning in the silver floor-length, one-shouldered crepe gown.

'How are you feeling?' Charlotte asked.

'Excited. And I think you should pour us a glass of bubbles while we wait for Gus to get here.'

'Gus is meeting you here?'

'Yes, we're going together. It's a second marriage for both of us so we aren't following rules that were set hundreds of years ago.'

Charlotte went to the champagne in the ice bucket Diane had pointed to.

'Do you mind opening it?' Diane asked. 'I might be happy, but I'm still shaking a little.'

Charlotte smiled, strangely glad that Diane wasn't entirely composed after all. Charlotte popped the champagne and poured them both a glass.

'To second chances,' Diane said and touched Charlotte's glass lightly.

Charlotte took a sip of champagne.

'Do you mind if I ask you something?'

'Of course not,' Diane said.

'It's a rather personal question.'

'They're the best kind.' Diane smiled.

'How did you know you were ready to marry Gus? After Ben's father died, I mean?'

'Ah. I'm sure Tim loved you and, because he loved you, I'm sure he would want you to find love again.'

'He would. I know he would. We had time to talk before he… Anyway, I know he would want me to be happy. Find someone, have a family. Have the life we planned. That isn't it.'

'Then?'

'I don't want to be hurt again. I don't want to feel that again. I'm scared.'

Charlotte tasted salt in her mouth but swallowed the tears back down. She refused to burst into tears on someone's shoulder half an hour before they were due to walk down the aisle.

'I think Ben loves you and I promise you there is no man more loyal, more loving.'

Charlotte nodded. 'None of that's in doubt. I know he is.'

Diane looked at her. 'Is it about yesterday? At the beach?'

Charlotte wanted to say no but couldn't bring herself to lie.

'It must have been awful, watching it. I'm so glad I wasn't there and only had to hear about it once we knew everyone was all right.'

'I could hardly breathe. I thought I'd lost him,' Charlotte admitted.

'But you didn't.'

For a moment Charlotte's whole world had stopped. It was such an awful and familiar feeling.

There was a knock at the door and Gus said, 'Honey, may I come in?'

'Yes, yes. Charlotte and I were just having a nerve settler.'

Gus came in and Charlotte felt like an intruder, though it was clear neither Diane nor Gus cared as they only had eyes for one another.

'Do you need anything else?' Charlotte asked.

'No, you go on. But just one thing.' Diane took Charlotte's arm. 'Think of this. If you don't see Ben again you lose him anyway. Is that what you want? It seems to me that your heart is going to be broken anyway, so why not take a chance?'

Charlotte nodded and attempted her best smile.

That logic would make sense if Ben loved her, she thought as she made her way down to the beach where the ceremony was to take place.

But Ben just kept telling her that their friendship was the most important thing. More important than sex. And desire. And lust. Maybe.

More important than intimacy? Than staring at one another across the pillow in the semi-darkness? More important than holding one another's hands in public, or announcing their relationship on the socials?

Maybe all those things were important.

Before she knew it, and before she was even sure she was meant to be there, Charlotte was at the beach.

Ben didn't want to risk their friendship for all those other things.

Or maybe he just didn't want to lose it.

Did that mean he didn't love her, or did it just mean he was scared too?

CHAPTER TWELVE

CHARLOTTE HELD BACK from the beach and watched the wedding crowd from a distance. Chairs were set out, decorated with green leaves and bright orange and red tropical blooms. A circle of flowers lay before the chairs, where the celebrant stood, waiting. Brightly coloured umbrellas stood around, providing partial shade. Some of the guests also held pretty parasols, to keep the sun away.

Ben stood to the left of the celebrant, next to Will. Her stomach tightened. Maybe it wasn't too late to change her mind and leave.

Ben wore long trousers and a white shirt, open at the collar and with the sleeves rolled up. He looked edible. Her heart soared and broke at once to look at him.

How could it hurt so much to lose something she never really had?

How could four years of beautiful friendship be ruined in one crazy week?

She willed her legs to carry her forward. When

she moved closer, Ben looked in her direction. Charlotte froze. He smiled gently and nodded, but didn't make a move towards her, for which she was grateful. Charlotte took one of the chairs furthest away from Ben. Once seated, she noticed Summer seated up closer, but she didn't move. This was a family occasion and Charlotte was just a friend.

Thankfully, Diane and Gus arrived arm in arm soon after. The guests stood, and even though Charlotte had already seen Diane and Gus dressed for the wedding, she still felt tears welling up. By the time they were saying their vows her face was wet and by the time they kissed she'd wet a whole tissue. She looked around and gratefully noticed she wasn't the only one shedding a tear. Though she didn't dare look in Ben's direction. She might start howling.

If you couldn't cry at a wedding, then when could you cry?

She felt guilty that they weren't entirely happy tears. Some of the tears were because she was witnessing the triumph of hope over loss, seeing someone take this leap again and find great love for a second time. But most of Charlotte's tears were because she didn't think she could do that same thing, because after yesterday and last night the thought of committing her life to another person felt further away than ever.

It was Ben she wanted.

It was Ben she wanted to marry. Ben's babies she wanted to carry. Ben's arms she wanted to lie in every night.

But what if something terrible happened to him too?

That was even assuming he would one day share her feelings. She didn't think she was strong enough or brave enough to do what Diane and Gus were doing now and that was why the tears kept falling, steadily, but quietly. Thankfully, most eyes were facing forward to Diane and Gus. She turned her head away from the direction Ben was standing.

When the ceremony was over, the guests followed the bride and groom to a table where champagne was being poured. Charlotte watched Ben follow his mother and new stepfather over with their families. Photos were being taken, but Charlotte was certainly not going to be a part of that. She stayed out of the way and sat on a bench and looked out over the water while she waited.

It would also give her face a chance to recover. Her skin was still tight from the tears, and probably looked a mess. She was thankful she'd nearly given up on make-up since being in Bali as the humidity made it slide right off anyway.

She felt someone behind her and knew it was Ben even before she turned. Of course she did. She now had a sixth sense as far as he was concerned. Was this what her life would be like from now on? Her being acutely aware of his presence, feeling him in her bones, needing him, wanting every moment, while his heart remained untouched, immune?

Yes. That was what it would be like.

There was no way she could keep seeing him casually, just be friends.

But it was that or lose him entirely.

Would friendship be enough? Would it even be *possible*?

'Thank you for staying.'

'I… I was being rash. I shouldn't have said I'd leave.'

'Charlotte, I'm sorry.' Ben bowed his head.

'What on earth for? I'm the one who should be sorry.' She'd come to Bali to support her best friend, instead she'd let her feelings run away from her.

'I'm sorry for making you come to a wedding.'

She laughed. 'What? Why? It was a beautiful wedding. I'm glad I came.'

'But you cried.'

She looked down. So he had seen.

'Yeah, well, I've been doing that a bit lately.'

He nodded, but he didn't look happy. 'I know it must remind you of Tim.'

'Tim? Why? Because it's a wedding?' Not this again. No matter how many times she tried to get him to understand, he didn't see that it wasn't about Tim, at least not directly.

'Because you two didn't make it down the aisle.'

Then, because she didn't think what the gesture might mean or do to her senses, she stood up, walked to Ben, and picked up his hand. She intended to reassure him that this wasn't the case but it quickly became more. Because as soon as her skin touched his, she wanted more. She wanted to slide her hand up his bare forearm and all around him. She wanted to press herself against him. And never, ever let go.

'I wasn't thinking of Tim when I cried.'

'You weren't?'

'No. I was thinking of you.'

'Me?'

Charlotte's hand was still in his, but it was her words that touched him most. 'Why?'

'Because…because I don't know what to do about us. Because I'm terrified. And confused.'

Charlotte hadn't been crying over Tim, but over him. Ben Watson.

Could his annoying big brother be right? Could he have missed all the signs because he was stupidly hung up on the idea that Charlotte wasn't over Tim, or that she wasn't ready to move on?

Yes, he could have. Believing he was second best. Believing he was Charlotte's fallback.

'You don't have to be scared,' he said, and she gave him a withering look. He knew that look, because he knew Charlotte and he could tell that she was biting back a sharp retort.

One he would deserve, because he hadn't given her anything to feel secure about. He'd been keeping his own feelings hidden and disguised. He'd been purposefully keeping the full extent of his emotions from her so as not to frighten her. And he realised he might have gone too far.

Ben might be able to guess what Charlotte was thinking by that look, but she couldn't read his mind. Especially not when he'd been trying so hard and for so long to keep his true feelings hidden. He was so practised in denying them even from himself.

'I love you, Charlotte.' Her eyes widened and he got the feeling she was actually going to argue with him. 'And no, not as your friend. Well, as your friend, but as your everything. Your lover, your partner. Your boyfriend. And your best friend.'

Charlotte's mouth opened and closed several times as she searched for the words.

He stepped in and kissed her lips instead. For a second, she paused but then answered him with an unambiguous kiss. She surged towards him, grabbed him and pulled him to her. It wasn't the way you kissed someone if you were ambivalent or wavering. His heart soared, desire kicked in and he pulled her closer, deeper.

She drew back just enough to take a breath. 'I love you too,' she whispered. Everything around him stopped and there was only Charlotte, standing before him. He let the words sink in. 'And not just as a friend. But as my everything.'

Her face was still a little flushed but her eyes were bright. And maybe a little glassy. She'd never been more beautiful. Now he struggled for the words.

'I love you,' he tried the words again. Unfamiliar on his tongue. 'As my everything.'

She hugged him.

He felt her shaking.

She was crying. Again?

He pulled her back to wipe away her tears and reassure her that everything would be all right, but she wasn't crying, she was laughing. He wanted to swat her.

'What's so funny?' he asked.

'This! Us! We're idiots.'

'Not idiots just…'

'Lovesick fools? I was scared. So scared,' she admitted.

He took her hand and led her back to the bench she'd been sitting on earlier. They sat, facing away from the curious eyes of the wedding guests.

'I was so scared, I'm still so scared. Not just about what if something happens to you, but what if you change your mind?' she said.

He cupped her cheeks in his hands.

'Why would I do that?'

'Because…because people do.'

'Are you worried *your* feelings will change?'

She shook her head adamantly. 'No.'

'Why not?'

'Because I know you, I've been getting to know you for four years now and I know you inside and out. But why are you so sure?'

'My feelings didn't change this week.' Even as the words came out, he still wasn't sure he was going to say them. 'I have *always* loved you.'

Charlotte let go of his hand.

'Define always,' she whispered. Since a month ago, a year ago…what was he saying?

'Always. Since the first day we met. Since our first conversation about Picasso when you almost spilt champagne over me.'

'But…' Suddenly her mouth was too dry to make sounds.

'I have loved you since you told me about Tim. I have loved you since, since…always. And that's why I have been by your side for the past four years, listened to you talk about all your dates, watched you… After all that, I still love you. So, you see, I really don't think that there is anything you can do that will stop me loving you. Even if I wanted to.'

He gave her a lopsided grin, but Charlotte untangled herself from his arms.

He'd thought she'd be pleased, but she was annoyed.

'Always? All this time?'

This wasn't fair.

'You asked me—no, you made me promise—to tell you how I was feeling, but you kept this from me.'

'I didn't know how to tell you without scaring you. I didn't know how to say it without scaring myself.'

'Why? Ben, for the past few days I've been dying inside, thinking that you didn't love me. I've been thinking this has meant nothing to you.'

'It hasn't meant nothing, it's meant everything.'

But Charlotte's feelings went from desperate to furious.

'I nearly got on a plane! I nearly didn't speak to you again; I thought you didn't care.'

'No, Charlotte, I care.'

'You kept this from me.'

'Because I had to. For the sake of—'

'I know! Our friendship! I get it.'

Charlotte stood. But she didn't run.

There was no point. There was no part of the world she could run to where she could escape Ben. Because that would mean escaping her own feelings. Escaping herself.

Always. He'd always loved her. And she'd treated him like a girlfriend. She'd told him about the men she'd been with as if he were an indifferent... Nausea rose inside her. She'd hurt him. It had been unknowing, but she'd hurt him. Day after day.

'I didn't know, I'm sorry.'

'Of course you didn't know and you have nothing to be sorry for. Charlotte, I even tried to hide it from myself.'

'Why didn't you say something earlier?'

'Because I knew you weren't ready.'

The realisation dawned on her. Ben had been right. She might have accepted that Tim was gone, but she hadn't been ready to move on. Not last week, not a few days ago and certainly not yesterday. Not until this very moment had she been brave enough to tell Ben her true feelings.

'He's always going to be here. He's always going to be in my past. Ben, you need to accept that just as much as I do.'

'I realise that now. I know that Tim will always be in your past, but I intend to be in your future.'

Charlotte smiled at him, bursting with happiness.

He pulled her to him and cupped her chin in his hand. She fell into his beautiful sea-blue gaze and she stroked his newly shaven cheek.

'Is it because I shaved my beard off?' he asked.

'Yes. I mean no.'

He laughed.

'I saw you differently. As if for the first time.'

'So you don't like the beard?'

'I didn't say that. I just saw you anew. Afresh.'

One side of his lips lifted into a grin. Also a new look. Her stomach swooped.

'If I grow it again, will you still love me?'

She dragged a fingertip down his smooth skin.

'It wasn't just the beard. That was just when I realised I was attracted to you.'

'And?' Ben tilted his head.

'The attraction was one thing. It's pretty intense, as you might be able to tell, but it's also far more than that. I realised I want you to be my everything.'

He nodded.

She felt someone approach them and looked around to see Diane holding two glasses of champagne.

'We are about to do some speeches… We won't interrupt you, but I suspect you both might have something to celebrate as well.' She handed them both a glass.

Charlotte stood and hugged Diane. 'Congratulations, I'm so pleased for you both.'

Diane hugged her back tightly, then Ben hugged his mother as well.

She smiled at them both.

Ben took Charlotte's hand and they followed Diane over to where a string quartet was playing, filling the air and their hearts with the sound of violins, the exact way Charlotte had always dreamed.

EPILOGUE

CHARLOTTE'S HEART WAS RACING.

They would all be here in less than ten minutes.

She looked at Ben. He needed a haircut, but he'd had a shave. And his sweater didn't have any holes or stains. He still took her breath away.

She was wearing a new, loose-fitting dress and was happy with her appearance. Best of all Ben had tidied their apartment—formerly Ben's apartment. They had hardly needed to discuss that she would move into Ben's, given that his apartment was bigger and brighter than hers.

'Relax, there's nothing to worry about.'

'How are you relaxed? In five minutes our parents will get here. All of them!'

'Yes, and I'm excited.'

'Excited? What if they don't get along? What if it's a disaster?'

He pulled her to him. 'Then we have something to laugh about later.'

She pressed her cheek to his soft sweater.

Diane and Gus had arrived at Heathrow that

afternoon and were expected at Ben and Charlotte's apartment that evening for an early dinner.

A week ago, it had seemed like a great idea to invite Charlotte's parents as well. That way they would tell them their news all at once.

Now, it seemed like a silly idea. Diane and Gus would be tired, her parents…well, her parents would be delighted. That only made Charlotte more nervous—high expectations and all that.

'It's going to be fine. In fact, it will be more than fine. Do you honestly think your parents will be anything but delighted when we tell them? My mother's going to be beside herself. Gus too.'

'Gus will probably cry,' Charlotte conceded. 'If their wedding was anything to go by.'

'So, the only thing we really need is tissues.'

Dinner was ready and in the oven—prepared, of course, by Ben, with Charlotte his trainee sous chef. Champagne was in the fridge.

Ben picked up her hand. The ring, sapphire blue like the Balinese water, sparkled on her ring finger. She lifted herself up and kissed him. His lips were as soft and welcome as always, his arms as strong. She hugged him tight.

'Will they think we're rushing things?'

'First, I don't care, and second, we've known one another for years. I don't think we can be accused of rushing anything.'

'But we're not just engaged, we've set a date. In

two weeks' time!' Charlotte giggled. 'I guess it's at least more notice than your mother gave you.'

The plan was for Will and Summer to arrive just before the wedding. They were the only others who already knew Ben and Charlotte's plan for a whirlwind register-office wedding with a small party afterwards. They'd had to tell them so they could make their travel plans.

'Do you think your parents will be upset? You're their only daughter, maybe they want a bigger thing.'

Charlotte laughed. 'Dad will be delighted that all he has to do is turn up and Mum… Mum won't mind at all when she knows the reason we want to get married so quickly.' She gave Ben a knowing look.

'They'll think you're pregnant already.'

'I could be.' She grinned and Ben's mouth dropped.

She laughed. 'Kidding! But I want to start trying, you know that.'

Ben nuzzled the sensitive spot beneath her ear. 'We could start now. We don't have to wait until the wedding.'

Charlotte pulled him even tighter. She loved this man with all of her heart and could not wait to start living the rest of her life with him.

* * * * *